This book is for Terry
Her Sweetie-Head's
Super Hugger-Squeezer.

· INTRODUCTION ·
by Phil Foglio

Noted visionary and loon Charles Fort had a concept that he referred to as "Steam Engine Time".

For decades after James Watt made it a practical device, steam engines were used solely as water pumps. Steam powered vehicles were invented, but people seemed to be unable to grasp the applications. Napoleon attended a demonstration of a steam powered boat and remarked that he couldn't see any reason why a person would want to sail against the wind.

Fort believed that a radical concept cannot gain general acceptance until a critical number of people are familiar with the underlying principles. When that mysterious threshold is crossed, then everybody suddenly seems to realign with the underlying principle. When that threshold is crossed, then everybody realizes that steam can power ships, locomotives, automobiles, dirigibles, etcetera.

I believe that it is this theory that explains the comparative anonymity of Jon Hasting's brilliant comic, *Smith Brown Jones*. It is a superb book, utilizing well thought out science fictional concepts as its frame work, and then filling it to the brim with the best kind of slapstick. Its humor relies on excellent writing, fine timing, and a wonderfully energetic cartooning style.

People are not used to this. It is bizarre. Unheard of. A statistical anomaly. And statistical anomalies are supposed to be ignored, or else you'll be hit by a meteor, and trust me, that smarts.

Thus, by buying this book, you are helping to bring Humanity into a new age; "Smith Brown Jones Time". A glorious golden age for humorous science-fiction comics everywhere. A time when worthy creators like Jon will establish themselves on Best Seller Lists across the globe, bringing forth an era of peace, love and 100% literacy, and you, yes you, dear reader, are helping to make it happen!

So go! Buy as many copies of this book as you can! Mail it to your friends! Distribute it to schoolchildren! Send copies to random people overseas!

Let us hasten towards Paradise!

CHAPTER ONE

> Galactic Central Hub transmission #34-q12-864w
> To: Hub Accountancy Office, Records Division
> From: Accountant 1555-q, "Smith Brown Jones"
> Re: Official log entry #15/48/1555-q
>
> Message: "Another planetary rotation period, another distribution of a monetary unit."

THE PENTAGON
"Five Corners for Peace"

Mr. President,

   As per your request, we have secretly enlisted the finest theoretical minds available in order to formulate an overview of hostile actions alien life forms may take against our planet and, more importantly, our great nation. We sent questionnaires to prominent thinkers of all ilk; among them: physicists, anthropologists, astronomers, psychologists, sociologists and science fiction writers.

   The following brief is the tabulation of their theories and the Pentagon's recommendations concerning them.

   The project, entitled the Xenoform Malevolence Anticipation Strategy (X.M.A.S.), is presented here in summary form in two categories. First, modes of operation that alien hostiles could use. Second, suggested courses and strategies to counter these insurgent actions.

Wishing you good reading,

Gen. Bradley T. Walkins
Gen. Bradley T. Walkins
Extra-Secret Operations
Third Unmarked Door Past the Supply Closet
Second Floor, The Pentagon

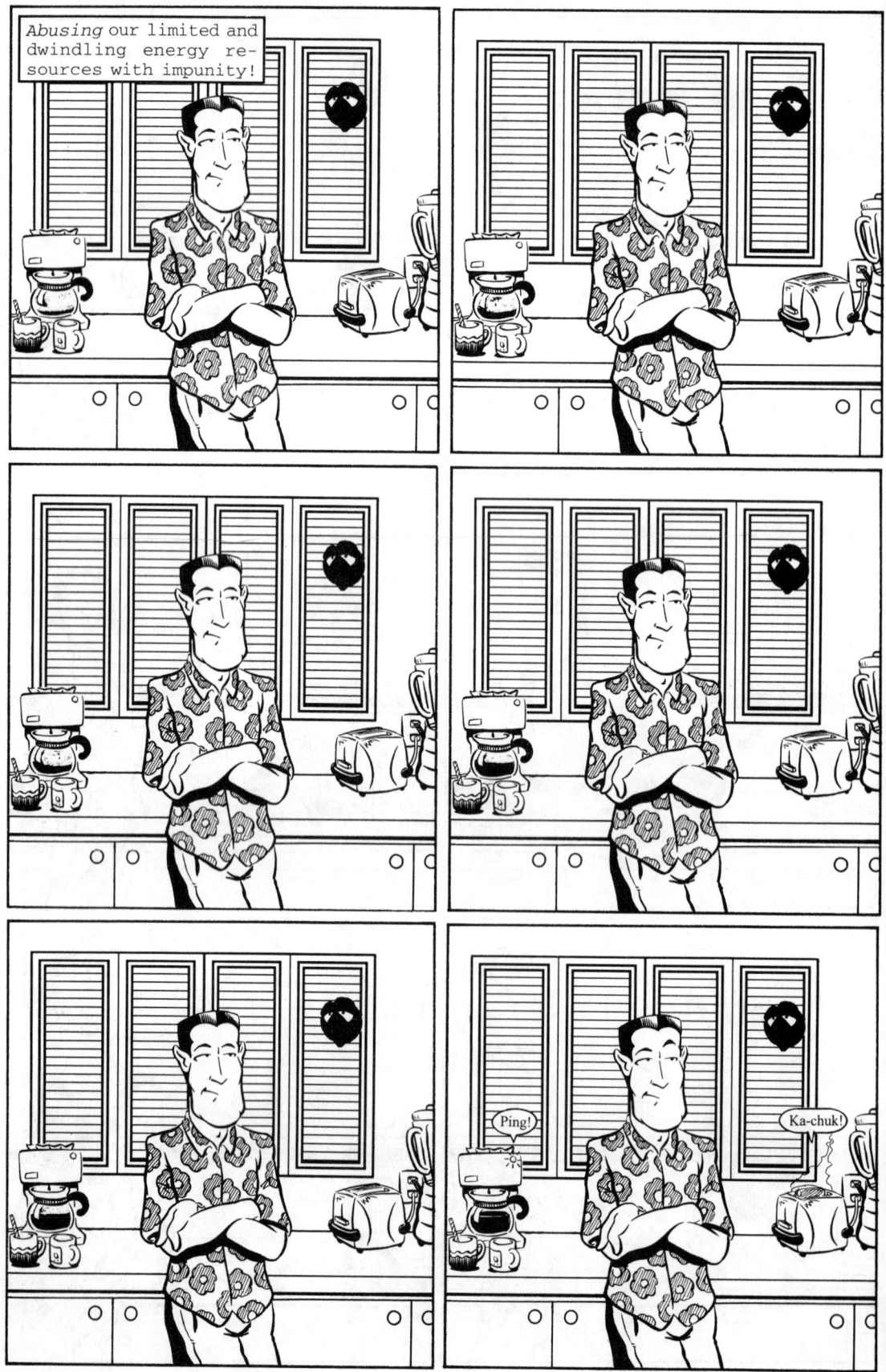

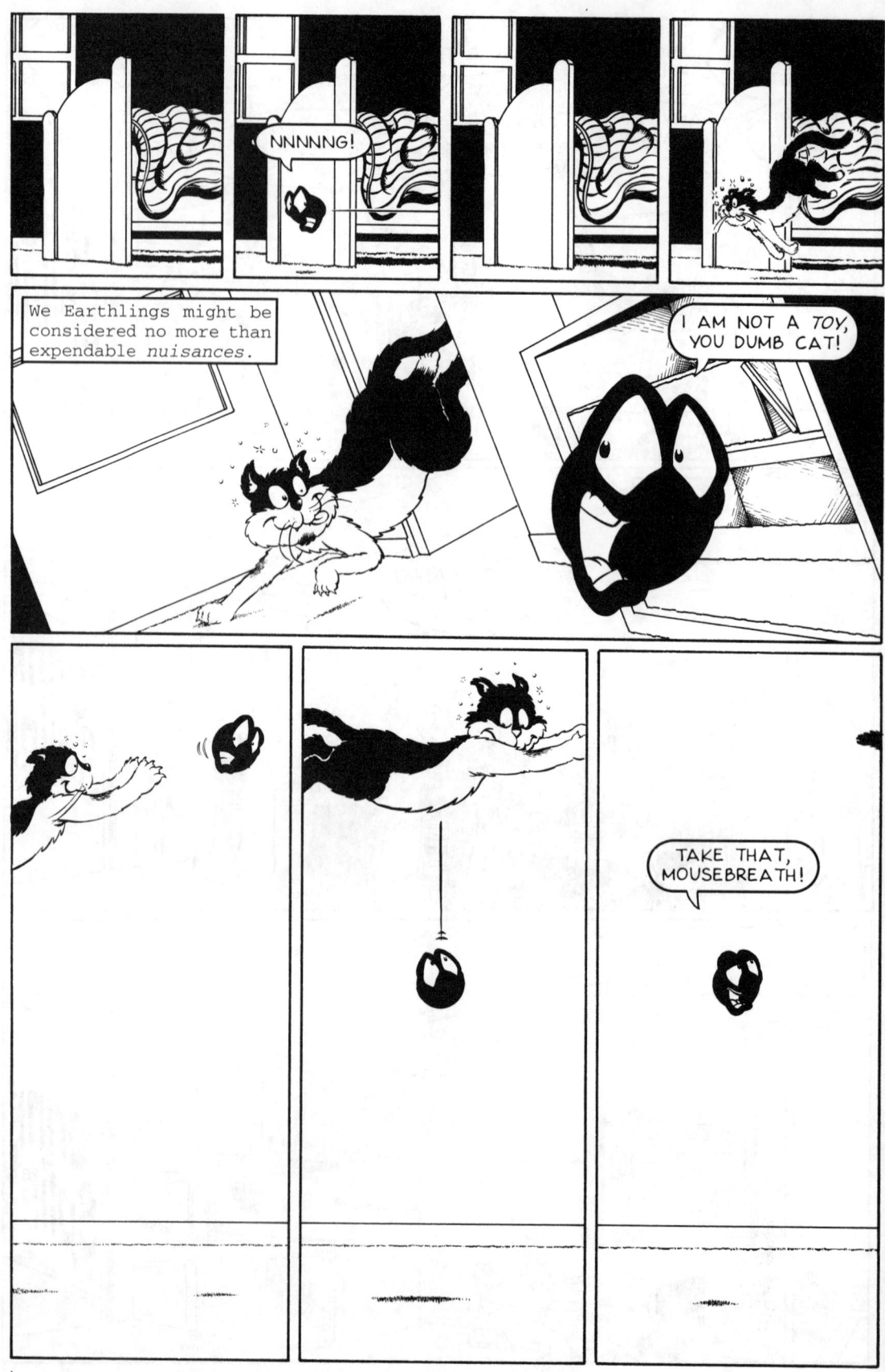

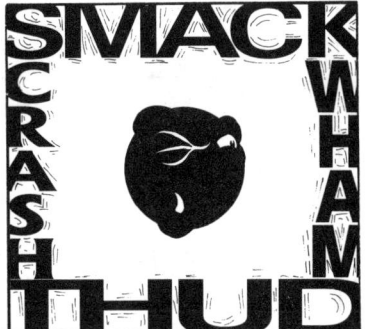

Next: Television, Robot Assassins and a Psycho Lizard Thing.

Chapter Two

Excerpt from the Galactic Central Hub's
Accountant Handbook,
Published by Grogil and Son.
Reprinted by permission

Introduction:
What does it mean to be an Accountant?
by Lower Sub-Assistant Fozzdink, Lord-high CPA, ret.

Congratulations! Having passed the rigorous and grueling induction test, you are now on your way to an exciting new life as a Galactic Central Hub Interplanetary Accountant!

But what exactly does that mean?

It means adventure! When you complete your training, you will be assigned to your very own planet! Once there, you will take into account that planet's potential for application into the Galactic Central Hub's Interstellar Congress!

It means job security! As you know, the Hub Accountancy Council researches each planet thoroughly, to find as-close-as-possible species matches for the accountants and their subjects. This allows the Accountant to move freely among those he/she/it is studying for a more accurate assessment of qualifying merits.

It means the latest technology! Since, for everyone's safety, no unauthorized off-world items are allowed, you will be assigned the latest in advanced accountancy equipment, the newly developed Peripherally Operating Personality System, or P.O.P.S. The P.O.P.S. unit will help you obtain accommodations, monetary units and other necessities while maintaining a low-profile. It will also act as your personal computer, information storage and retrieval unit and general friendly chum.

All in all, accountancy means a career you can be proud of! To help you, this informational handbook will detail everything you need to know about being a Galactic Central Hub Accountant, a job that makes the Galaxy a better place to exist in. Good luck and good accounting!

**All mirth &
no matter.**

DRINK IMBIBE AND COME ALIBE!
HE LOVES THAT DOG MORE 'AN ME!
I GOT MORE THAN YOU'LL EVER HAVE RIGHT HERE, GIRL! SO JUST KISS IT!
'N I GO "WORD, HOME-FRIES, MY PANTS IS SUPPOSED TO BE HALF-WAY DOWN!"
...THEN THE BEE FLIES RIGHT UP MY NOSE!
I HATE YOU!
I... I'M IN LOVE WITH YOUR SHOES. THE RED PUMPS... WITH THE BOWS!
BLEEP! BLEEP! BLEEPITY! BLEEP! BLEEP, BLEEP!!
CRASH! YOU STUPID... THUD... I'LL KILL YOU! ...SMACK...CRUNCH!
FZZZZZZ...
APEX!
IMBIBE
MILT
THWAP!
THWAP!
THWAP!
THWAP!
RRKKK!
THWAP!

KNOCK, KNOCK!
WHOIZZIT?
IT'S MEL AND CHUCK, MR. PHTANG.
HOLD ON!
GRRR!
SNARL!
ENTER!
WELL?!!
MEL AND I GOT THREE FROM *KELLY*, FOUR FROM *DEEP PROBE*, THREE FROM *MILT* AND TWO FROM *THE PHOEBE PFEIFFER SHOW*, MR. PHTANG.
TWELVE MORE, EXCELLENT! I BET THEY WERE *WRITHING* IN *AGONY*, THE HORRIBLE RE-ALIZATION OF THEIR *DARK FATE* PASTED ACROSS THEIR *TWISTED* VISAGES!

KNOW US HUMANS, FOR IT IS BY OUR HANDS THAT YOUR DOWNYFALL IS ASSURED-D-D! YOU RRR NOTHING-ING, WE RRR BY FAR-R-R YOUR P-POSTERIORS-S!
YOUR TRANSLATOR IS MALFUNCTIONING AGAIN, MR. PHTANG.
#@*!! STOOPID TRANSLA-LA-LATOR-OR! ERK SPUTTER
BAM! BAM! BAM!
2,4,6,8... WE WILL DOMINATE. THAT'S BETTER.
ENOUGH! IT IS TIME FOR MORE CLEANSING. GO, GO TO THE SHOW CALLED FRANCINE (FOUR P.M. ON MOST STATIONS) AND APPLY SOME REEKING VENGEANCE.
YES, SIR!
HA, HA, HA, HEE, HEE... HUMPH.
SLAM!
OH, HOW I WISH I COULD GO...
...BUT I SHALL BIDE MY TIME AS THE MASTER WISHES!
WHEN OUR VICTORY IS CERTAIN, THEN... THEN...
BWA-HA-HA-HA!
SIGH.

WHERE IS IT?
WHERE IS THE ROBOPROBOSCIS, WHERE IS IT?!
AHH-HA!
BEEP.
BEEP.
YES, YES.
THERE WE GO...
BEEP.
BING!
...AND DONE!
DING DONG!
WHAT THE...?! WHO COULD THAT BE?
I DON'T KNOW, BUT (OH BOY!) WE GET TO TAKE AN "ALTERNATE" ROUTE TO THE TV STUDIO!
IT'S *RAZ!*
RAZ, WHAT ARE YOU DOING HERE?
YOU'RE THE ONE WHO'S NOT SUPPOSED TO BE HERE. WHICH IS, IF I RECALL, WHY *I* HAD TO GO TO THE VET AND PICK UP MR. BUTANE.
HI RAZ.

THAT'S MY CAT?! I THOUGHT IT WAS A LAMP.
MEW.
SMITH, THE FUZZY FUNNEL HEAD CAN WAIT. LET'S GO!
WHERE YOU GOING? SOMEPLACE INTERESTING, I HOPE.
NOWHERE
ON THE *FRANCINE* SHOW!!
EXCUSE ME?!
THE *FRANCINE* SHOW!
THE MOST WATCHED TALK-SHOW ON THE PLANET?!
WELL... MIGHT AS WELL CALL THE PENTAGON AND HAVE THEM COME AND DISSECT YOUR THICK ALIEN SKULL AND SEE IF THERE IS *ANYTHING EVEN IN IT!*
YOU FINISHED?
NO!
RANT RAVE RANT RANT RAVE RAVE RAVE RAVE RANT RANT
THANKS, POPS.
OOPS.

CALM BLUE OCEAN, RAZ, CALM BLUE OCEAN.
BELIEVE ME, I'M THE *LAST* ONE WHO WANTS THEIR BRAINS NEATLY DOCUMENTED IN THE NATIONAL ARCHIVES.
HOW MUCH TIME, POPS.
THIRTY-TWO MINUTES.
-CLICK!
OK, THE TWO MINUTE SLIDE SHOW STARTS NOW.
ME
HUMANS
SINCE I RESEMBLE A HUMAN DRESSED UP LIKE AN ALIEN, MOST PEOPLE PAY ME NO NEVER MIND.
TV?
RESEARCH SHOWS MOST HUMANS *IGNORE* THE UNUSUAL. TO DEAL WITH IT WOULD TAKE PRECIOUS TIME AWAY FROM FIGURING OUT WHAT'S ON TV.
GOOD *LORD*, *CHOKE*!
BEER
HOWEVER, THE "LESS COUTH" TEND TO CARRY ON ABOUT INEXPLICABLE PHENOMENA, OF WHICH POPS, BEING BASICALLY A FLOATING *HEAD*, DEFINITELY IS.
TV?
BEER
THEREFORE, IF WE CAN CONVINCE THE LEGIONS OF STUPID PEOPLE THAT POPS IS NOT WHAT HE APPEARS TO BE...

...THEN EVERYBODY LIVES HAPPILY EVER AFTER.
THANKS POPS, YOU CAN STOP NOW.
GOOD, I WAS GETTING A HEADACHE.
YOU'RE A LOUSY REPORTER. I GOT THE "WHO", "WHAT", "WHERE", "WHY" AND "WHEN" BUT NO "HOW".
BY TAKING POPS ON A TALKSHOW.
NO ONE WILL BELIEVE HE'S ANYTHING MORE THAN A PUBLICITY STUNT.
CLICK
BLINK BLINK
C'MON POPS.
WE'LL BE BACK IN TIME FOR PRACTICE IF YOU WANT TO HANG OUT HERE. SEE YOU SOON...AND STOP FROWNING!
YOU GET YOUR DUMB BUTT KILLED AND YOU CAN'T BE IN THE BAND ANYMORE!
WHAT, AND LET YOU HAVE *ALL* THE SOLOS?!

I AM... A LARGE... RHINO'S BOTTOM ...WITH AN... ITTY-BITTY... BRAIN!
...AND YOU MAY HAVE FRONT ROW SEATS, SIRS.
KIWI-TV HOME OF Francine
STAGE 12
SNURK!
AND... YOU MAY... HAVE FRONT-ROW... SEATS, SIRS!
MAKE HIM SAY "THESE AREN'T THE DROIDS WE'RE LOOKING FOR," CHUCK.
SHUT UP, OR HE'LL COME TO, MEL!
I'LL COME TO... WHAT THE...?!
PERHAPS WE'LL JUST WAIT AROUND BACK, MEL.
FINE IDEA, CHUCK.

GOOD GAWD!
JUMP BACK! WANNA KISS MYSELF!
TAKE IT TO DA BRIDGE!
PING!
PING!
PING!
PING!
PING!
PING!
PING!
PING!
@%$#!! THIS IS *NOT* MY DAY! I THOUGHT YOU FIXED THE BLASTED CLOAKING DEVICE!
I *DID*, YOU'RE THE ONE WHO PUT THE JAMES BROWN CD IN IT! THE CD PLAYER IS *ABOVE* THE CLOAKING DEVICE, REMEMBER?!

I'M SUPER BAD..ERRK!
PING!
PING!
PING!
PING!
PING!
MAD
THERE, THAT'S BETTER.
PING!
KWLTV
JUST IN TIME, TOO.
PARK
IN YOU GO AND WE'RE OFF TO STARDOM.
WHERE COULD THIS JONES MORON BE!
THE MORON IS HERE, SIR!
MOVE IT! WE'RE ON IN THIRTY SECONDS.
OK, THE RULES: SMILE, DON'T SWEAR, DON'T SCRATCH INAPPROPRIATE PLACES, DON'T BEAT THE HECK OUT OF PEOPLE WITH OPPOSING VIEWPOINTS AND NEVER, EVER, FOR ANY REASON, TOUCH FRANCINE. GOOD LUCK.

Francine
CLAP
CLAP
CLAP
CLAP
AND NOW HERE'S THE LADY WHO GOT TO THE *TOP* BY GETTING TO THE *BOTTOM* OF IT...
FRANCINE!
HELLO, EVERYBODY!
THE ALIEN PRESENCE, UFOS, CLOSE ENCOUNTERS, LITTLE GREEN MEN.
ALL PART OF OUR FASCINATION WITH OTHERWORLDLY INTELLIGENCE.
BUT... DO THEY EXIST? HAVE ALIENS BEEN TO EARTH? ARE THEY HERE RIGHT NOW?
SOME SAY "NO". BUT THERE ARE A GROWING NUMBER WHO SAY "OH, YES, ABSOLUTELY." WE HAVE A FEW OF THEM HERE TODAY.
SO, ONCE AGAIN LET'S FIND OUT...
...WHAT IS THIS CRAP!

Panel 1:

Host: OUR FIRST GUEST, ENID MILLER, CLAIMS SHE WAS *ACTUALLY* ABDUCTED BY ALIEN BEINGS AND THEY DID ALL SORTS OF YUCKY, *GROSS* THINGS TO HER. PLEASE TELL US ABOUT YOURSELF.

Enid: WELL, I WAS *ACTUALLY* ABDUCTED BY ALIEN BEINGS...

...AND THEY DID ALL SORTS OF YUCKY, GROSS THINGS TO ME.

Panel 2:

Host: UH...YEAH. OUR NEXT GUEST, FRED LUMOX HAS A MASTERS DEGREE IN ALIEN BEHAVIOR AND INFILTRATION. MR. LUMOX...?

Fred: THE NAME IS *LOMUX*, NOT LUMOX.

ANYWAY, I BELIEVE THAT ALIENS ARE AMONG US *RIGHT NOW*, *SAPPING* OUR *WILLS* SO THAT WE MAY BECOME *GIANT BEVERAGE CONTAINERS* FULL OF *YUMMY BLOOD* FOR THEIR *INSATIABLE THIRSTS!*

Panel 3:

Host: OUR THIRD GUEST, MR. SMITH BROWN JONES, CLAIMS TO REALLY *BE* AN ALIEN FROM A FAR DISTANT GALAXY. MR. JONES...?

Mr. Jones: I'M AN ALIEN, NO DOUBT ABOUT IT. JUST *LOOK* AT ME, FOR CRIPES SAKE!

NOTHING SAYS "ALIEN BEING" LIKE GREEN SKIN AND POINTY EARS!

Panel 4:

Host: AND LASTLY, WE HAVE MRS. MARY HAROLD, WHO WAS SUPPOSED TO BE ON OUR "CELEBRITY VEGETABLE LOOK-ALIKE" SHOW BUT WAS MIS-BOOKED. MRS. HAROLD?

Mrs. Harold: THIS POTATO I GREW LOOKS LIKE NEWSCASTER WALTER CRONKITE, NOW RETIRED.

Mr. Jones: WOULD THAT MAKE IT A COMMEN-TATER, MARY?

Mrs. Harold: OH MR. JONES! *SNICKER*

LET'S OPEN IT UP WITH A QUESTION. WHAT DO ALIENS LOOK LIKE?
WELL, THEY CERTAINLY DON'T LOOK LIKE HIM!
ONLY THE HANDSOME ONES, FOLKS.
YOU HAVE A COMMENT, MA'AM?
YEAH, I AGREE WITH THE NERDY FELLA. THE GREEN GUY DON'T JIBE WITH MOST ALIEN DESCRIPTIONS I'VE HEARD.
ENID, MAYBE YOU HAVE SOME INSIGHT. DID YOU GET A LOOK AT YOUR ALIEN ABDUCTORS?
WELL, NOT REALLY.
BUT THEY DID ALL SORTS OF YUCKY, GROSS THINGS TO ME. IT'S ALL IN MY NEW BOOK! $19.95 AT FINE BOOKSTORES.
THEY DID ALL SORTS OF YUCKY GROSS THINGS TO ME!
ENID MILLER
THEY'RE EVIL! THEY HAVE AN ANTARCTIC BASE FROM WHICH THEY MANIPULATE WORLD LEADERS AND BREED US LIKE LIVESTOCK!
WE DO NOTHING OF THE SORT. IN FACT, WE HAVE CUTE, FRIENDLY ROBOTS.
I AM POPS. I AM FROM OUTER SPACE. SALUTATIONS TO ALL ON PLANET EARTH!
SEE?
OH! CUTE!

I'M SORRY, BUT MR. JONES NOR HIS CUTE ROBOT SEEM CAPABLE OF DOING YUCKY, *GROSS* THINGS TO ANYONE!
POPS, SAY "HELLO" TO OUR NEW, UPTIGHT FRIEND.
HELLO, UPTIGHT FRIEND.
HE'S JUST THE *SWEETEST* LITTLE THING.
NOT LIKE THE ALIENS IN MY BOOK!
THERE IS *NO WAY* THIS *CHARLATAN* IS AN ALIEN!
WOULD YOU LIKE TO MEET MR. CRONKITE?
HIYA, WALT!
THEY DID ALL SORTS OF YUCKY GROSS THINGS TO ME! ENID MILLER
$19.95. FINE BOOKSTORES.
AND *THAT* IS *NOT* A ROBO...OOPS.
GNN!
WALTER! COME BACK!
ENID MILLER

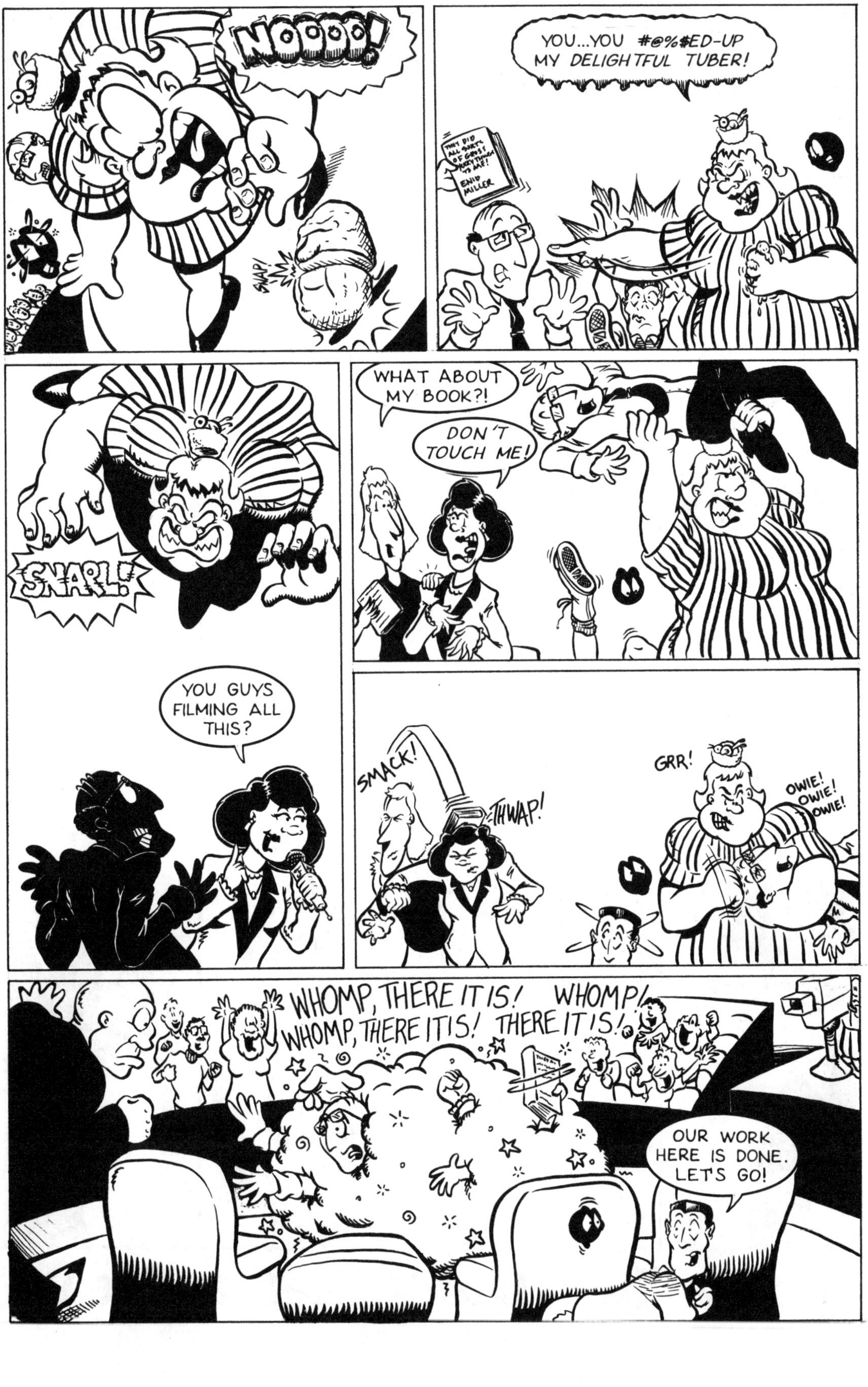

Next: They Don't Get a Break.

Chapter Three

The Chase is on!

Excerpt from the Galactic Central Hub's
Accountant Handbook,
Published by Grogil and Son.
Reprinted by permission

Chapter 54, Subsection 32:
Work Environment

Aside from the major duty as an information gatherer, all Hub Accountants are also responsible for maintaining a pristine work environment at all times.

The discovery, reporting and removal of any non-indigenous beings from your assigned planet is of utmost importance and it is vital to your success that you avoid outside contamination and/or subjugation of your research subjects.

The majority of the time, any off-worlders you have contact with will more than likely be lost tourists trying to find their way back to Hub designated space-traffic routes. In this case, be friendly and courteous. Try to help them get on their way as expediently as possible.

If the interlopers display a more insidious nature, contact the Hub Main Accountancy Office immediately (to avoid "prank" calls, separate voice-print clearance codes have been assigned to you and your P.O.P.S. unit, both must be given to activate the emergency communications uplink [WARNING: For crisis procedure ONLY!!]). Your supervisors will then work with you to promptly evaluate the situation, and put things right once again. Remember, a tidy work site is a happy work site!

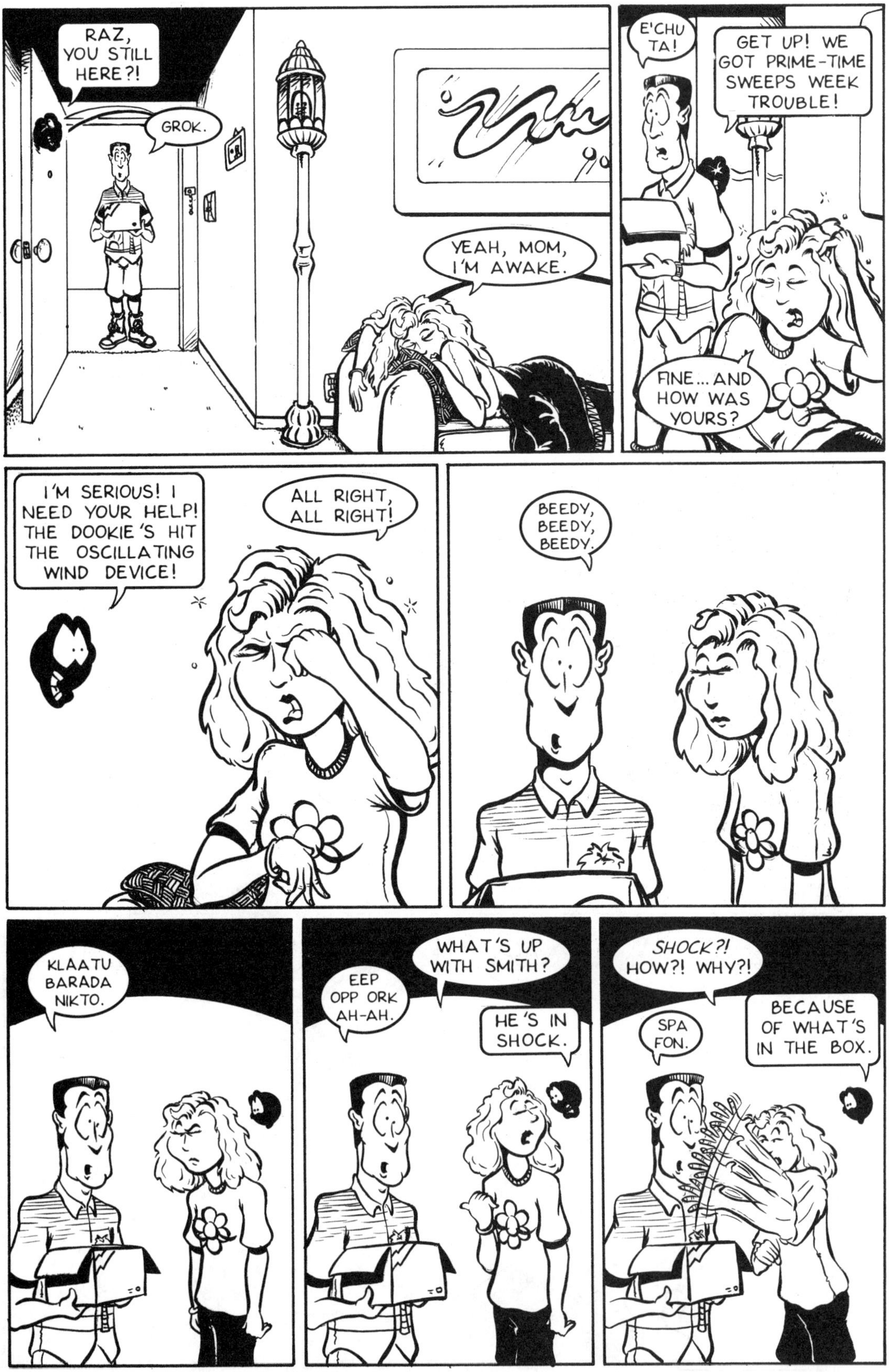
RAZ, YOU STILL HERE?!
GROK.
YEAH, MOM, I'M AWAKE.
E'CHU TA!
GET UP! WE GOT PRIME-TIME SWEEPS WEEK TROUBLE!
FINE... AND HOW WAS YOURS?
I'M SERIOUS! I NEED YOUR HELP! THE DOOKIE'S HIT THE OSCILLATING WIND DEVICE!
ALL RIGHT, ALL RIGHT!
BEEDY, BEEDY, BEEDY.
KLAATU BARADA NIKTO.
EEP OPP ORK AH-AH.
WHAT'S UP WITH SMITH?
HE'S IN SHOCK.
SHOCK?! HOW?! WHY?!
SPA FON.
BECAUSE OF WHAT'S IN THE BOX.

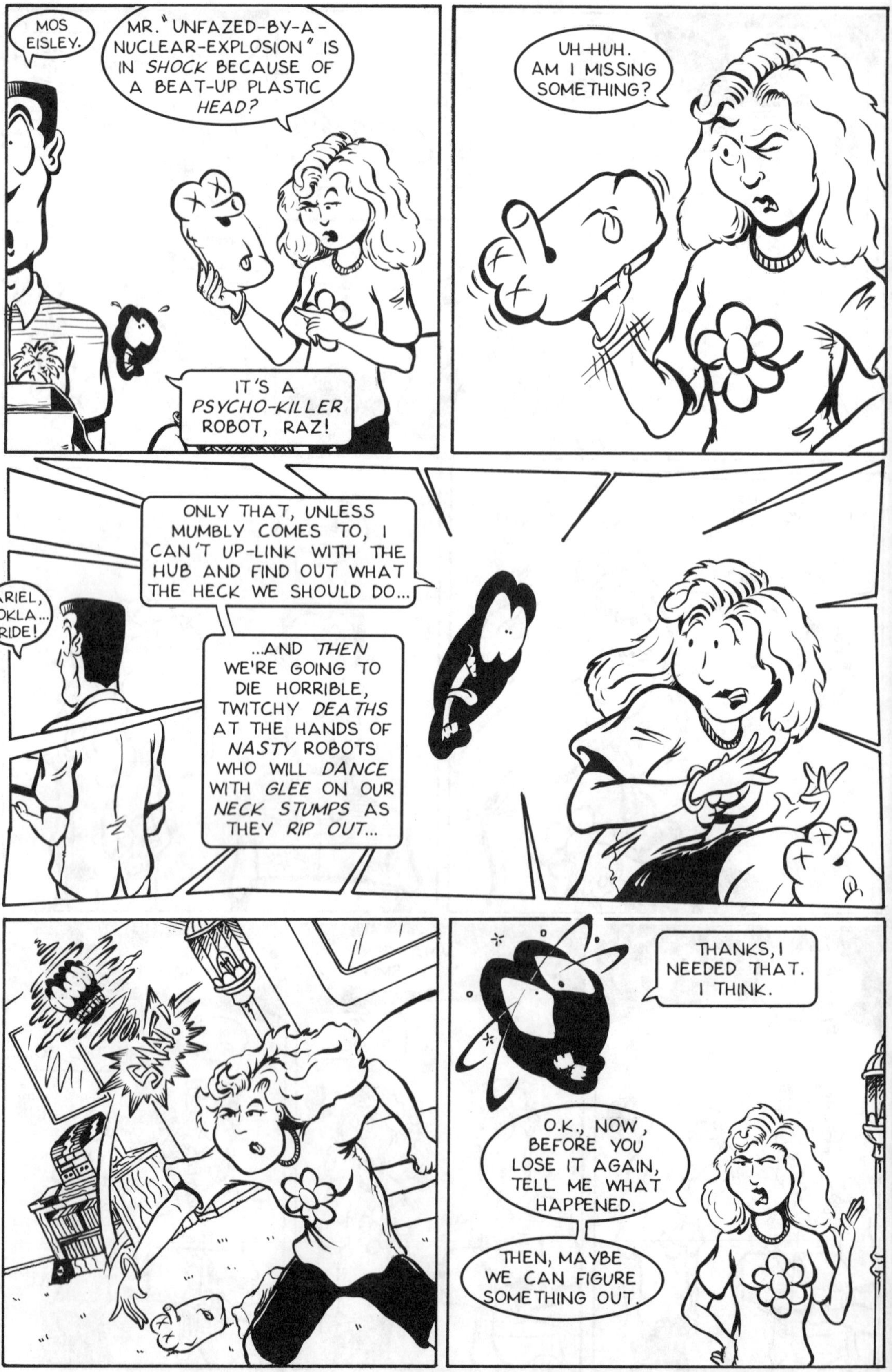
MOS EISLEY.
MR. "UNFAZED-BY-A-NUCLEAR-EXPLOSION" IS IN *SHOCK* BECAUSE OF A BEAT-UP PLASTIC *HEAD?*
IT'S A *PSYCHO-KILLER* ROBOT, RAZ!
UH-HUH. AM I MISSING SOMETHING?
ONLY THAT, UNLESS MUMBLY COMES TO, I CAN'T UP-LINK WITH THE HUB AND FIND OUT WHAT THE HECK WE SHOULD DO...
ARIEL, OOKLA... RIDE!
...AND *THEN* WE'RE GOING TO DIE HORRIBLE, TWITCHY *DEATHS* AT THE HANDS OF *NASTY* ROBOTS WHO WILL *DANCE* WITH *GLEE* ON OUR *NECK STUMPS* AS THEY *RIP OUT*...
SMAK!
THANKS, I NEEDED THAT. I THINK.
O.K., NOW, BEFORE YOU LOSE IT AGAIN, TELL ME WHAT HAPPENED.
THEN, MAYBE WE CAN FIGURE SOMETHING OUT.

KEEPIN' UP WITH THE JONES

"IT ALL STARTED WHEN WE WERE ACCOSTED AS WE LEFT THE *FRANCINE* SHOW. FORTUNATELY, SMITH WAS QUICK ON HIS FEET..."

"*LOOK!!* A TRANSVESTITE NUN FONDLER AND THE ELVIS IMPERSONATORS WHO LOVE HIM!"

"UH-OH, MEL."

"WOO WOO!"

"UH-OH, INDEED, CHUCK."

"INFO!"

"ACCESSING:...THEY'RE... MODIFIED STEALTH-BOTS FROM THE GREEB SYSTEM."

THE GOOD NEWS IS THEY'RE CARRYING GOOZI-2000 CELLULAR DISRUPTERS.
HOW'S THAT GOOD?
THEY HAVEN'T SHOT US WITH THEM YET. MESSY.
AND NOW THE BAD NEWS...
I WANT TO SEE THIS ONE SQUIRM, MEL.
LIKE A WIGGLY WORM, ONLY MORE SO, CHUCK.
IS IT ME, OR ARE WE SPENDING EN-TIRELY TOO MUCH TIME IN BACK ALLEYS?
I HAVE A STRONG BELIEF THAT YOU DON'T WANT TO DO THIS. I'M AN ACCOUNTANT.
AND I'M A FAX MACHINE, BUDDY.
WHEN'D YOU GET THAT ATTACH-MENT, CHUCK?
SHUT UP, MEL.
WOW, COOL. A CRIME!

I MEAN... HALT THIS VILENESS PRONTO OR FACE THE MYSTERIOUS WRATH OF ENIGMAN!
WHO??
EXACTLY! I AM MYSTERY WRAPPED IN AN ENIGMA, LIGHTLY FROSTED WITH A CONUNDRUM!
I AM ENIGMAN!
ENIGMAN? THAT STARTS WITH AN "E". HOW COME THERE'S A "Q" ON YOUR CHEST?!
YEAH, HEROBOY.
ALL PART OF THE *MYSTERY!* ORCHESTRATED CONFUSION, WORKS EVERY TIME.
NOW, WHICH ONE OF YOU IS THE BAD GUY? I CAME IN LATE.
ISN'T THAT REALLY A SUBJECTIVE QUESTION?
I MEAN IN THIS SITUATION, NOT IN GENER...

HA! I LAUGH AT YOU LIKE TEN THOUSAND *INSANE* HYENAS!
YOU ARE ABSOLUTELY NO MATCH *WHAT-SO EVER* FOR THE CONCENTRATED *HUNK* OF *EVIL* THAT IS *ME!*
FOR AS LONG AS NAMBY-PAMBY "GOOD" SHALL FLOUNDER AROUND PITEOUSLY, I, HYPERBULLY, THE *ULTIMATE* EVIL IN ALL THE WORLD, SHALL AL-WAYS BE THERE!
OH, I GET IT. "HYPERBULLY", YOU TALK IN "*HYPERBOLE*".
CUTE.
MOCK ME NOT, OR I'LL GIVE YOU SUCH A PINCH!
NOW THEN FELLOW BADDIES, CONTINUE YOUR EXCEEDINGLY VILE BUSINESS!
I'D STICK AROUND, BUT I HAVE A TRILLION THINGS TO DO!

HEE, HEE!
ADD HIM TO THE LIST, CHUCK?
DEFINITELY ADD HIM TO THE LIST, MEL.
A-HEM!
AS I WAS TRYING TO EXPLAIN, I'M NOT AN EARTH ACCOUNTANT, I'M A GALACTIC CENTRAL HUB ACCOUNTANT.
SO, WHAT SAY YOU PACK UP AND GET OFF MY PLANET, DOUBLE TIME.
NOW WHAT?
THOSE OF US WITH BUTTS *GRUNT* ARE GETTING THEM THE HECK OUT OF HERE!
HE'S MINE, CHUCK!
BACK OFF, MEL!

GRRR, MEL.
GRRR, CHUCK.
GRRR, MEL!
SAY GOODNIGHT, GRACIE!
NO! DON'T TURN ME OFF! I'LL GET YOOOO...
CLICK
COME BACK HERE, YOU!
RNNGH!
ALL RIGHT, ALL RIGHT. WE SURRENDER!
DANG-RIGHT YOU DO, LAUGHING BOY!
HOW DO WE GET OUT OF THIS?
ACCESSING...

ANY*TIME* NOW.
OFF-BUTTON, NO, NEVER REACH IT...WEAKNESS, *COME ON*...
YOU'RE MINE NOW, CHUMP.
GOT IT!
GREEB STEALTH-BOT HEADS ARE SCREWED ON *COUNTER-CLOCK WISE* AND THEY HAVE A *LOCKING* TARGET-TRACKING SYSTEM!
WHOOPIE FOR THEM. HOW DOES THAT HELP...
WELL, DUH, JONES!
NOW THEN, IF YOU'LL...WHAT ARE YOU SMILING ABOUT, HUB LACKEY?

AAAAAAAAAAAAAAAAAAAAAAAAAARR!
URK...
HEY, IT WORKED!
"HEY, IT WORKED!"?, "HEY, IT WORKED!"?
YOU WEREN'T SURE ABOUT THAT.
HE VERY WELL MIGHT HAVE...
I COULD BE...
YOU DIDN'T KNOW IF...
...URK.
...AND THAT'S WHY HE'S IN SHOCK.
I DON'T BLAME HIM.
HOW DID YOU GET BACK HERE?
TWONKY
I REVIVED ENIGMAN, BUT HE'D ONLY PUT THE HEAD IN THE BOX BEFORE HE STAGGERED OFF.
I CORRALLED SMITH INTO THE CAR AND DROVE US HOME. NOT AN EASY TASK; THE STEERING WHEEL TASTES AWFUL.
ACME

SHAZBOT!

HUMPH. WELL, IF SMITH'S BRAIN IS ANYTHING LIKE A HUMAN'S, THERE'S NO TELLING HOW LONG HE'LL BE LIKE THIS.

THE BRAIN CHEMISTRY IS ALMOST IDENTICAL, SO YOU'RE RIGHT.

WELL, LET'S GET HIM SITTING, I'VE GOT AN IDEA.

SQUA TRONT.

HEY, WHAT ABOUT THE OTHER ROBOT? WHAT IF SOMEONE FINDS HIM OR HIS GUN?

NO ONE'S GOING TO FIND THEM. AFTER THE FIGHT, THEY WERE GONE.

GONE? BUT DIDN'T YOU SAY THIS ONE TURNED OFF THE OTHER ROBOT?

YUP, IT DIDN'T MOVE ON ITS OWN POWER.

SO, SOMEONE MUST HAVE TAKEN HIM.

HARZACH

YES, BUT THE QUESTION IS...

...WHO WOULD BE DUMB ENOUGH TO WALTZ INTO A VERITABLE COMBAT ZONE AND MAKE OFF WITH A TWO-HUNDRED POUND KILLER ROBOT?

THIS IS SO COOL!

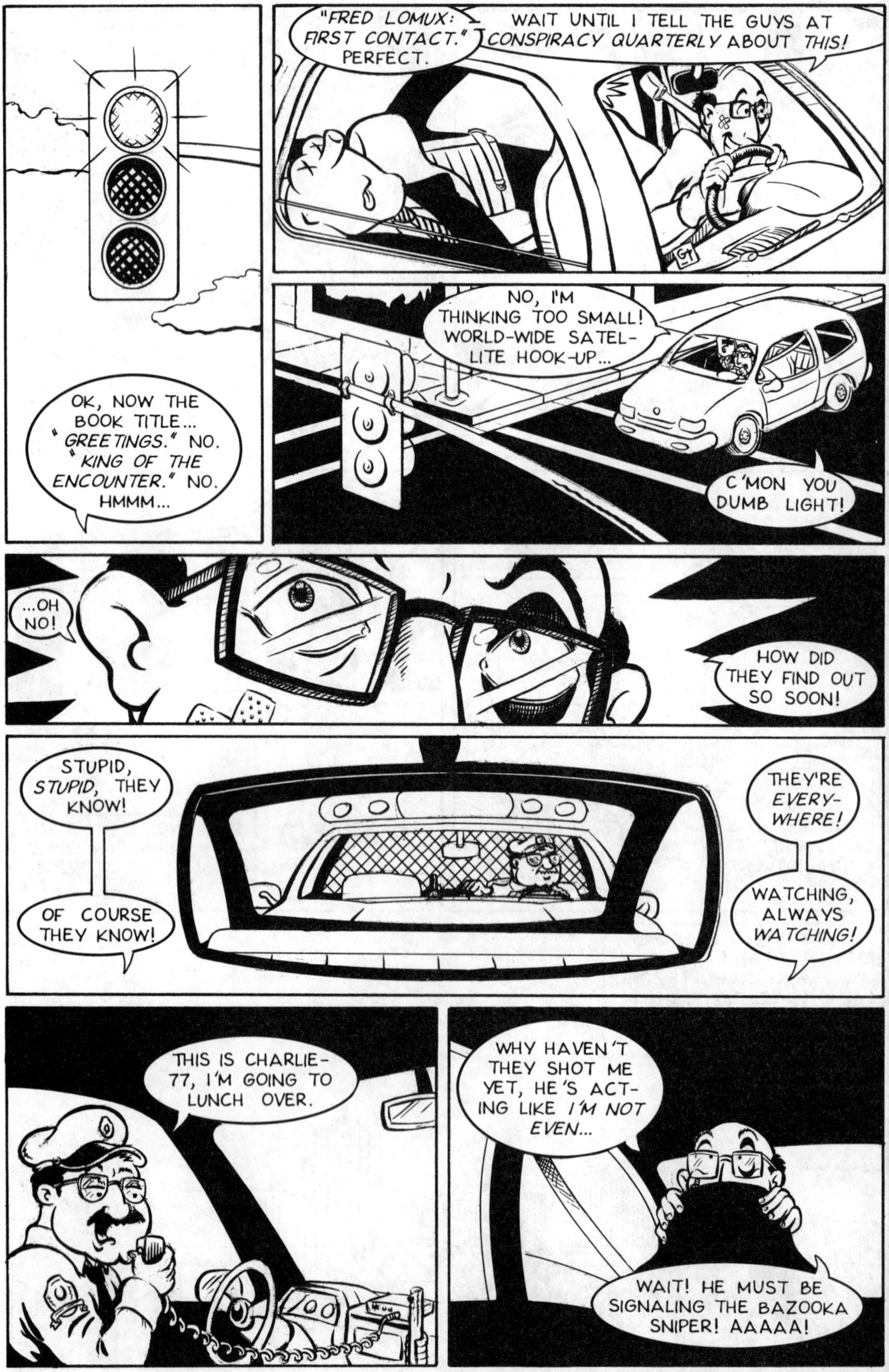
"FRED LOMUX: FIRST CONTACT." PERFECT.
WAIT UNTIL I TELL THE GUYS AT CONSPIRACY QUARTERLY ABOUT THIS!
OK, NOW THE BOOK TITLE... "GREETINGS." NO. "KING OF THE ENCOUNTER." NO. HMMM...
NO, I'M THINKING TOO SMALL! WORLD-WIDE SATEL-LITE HOOK-UP...
C'MON YOU DUMB LIGHT!
...OH NO!
HOW DID THEY FIND OUT SO SOON!
STUPID, STUPID, THEY KNOW!
OF COURSE THEY KNOW!
THEY'RE EVERY-WHERE!
WATCHING, ALWAYS WATCHING!
THIS IS CHARLIE-77, I'M GOING TO LUNCH OVER.
WHY HAVEN'T THEY SHOT ME YET, HE'S ACT-ING LIKE I'M NOT EVEN...
WAIT! HE MUST BE SIGNALING THE BAZOOKA SNIPER! AAAAA!

GOTTA GET OUT OF HERE!
WHAT THE...?!
FRANK'S FRANKS
AAAAAAAAAAAAAAAAAAAA
AAAAAAAAAAAAAAAAAAAAAAAAAAAA
RRRRRRRTT!!
WHEW!
POW
DINK.

THIS IS CHARLIE-77, POSSIBLE 5150, I NEED AN AMBULANCE TO 34TH AND VINE.
WHAT! I THOUGHT YOU WERE GOING TO LUNCH?
THEY CAN'T HAVE HIM!
MINE.
MINE!
MINE!
HELP ME! WE'VE GOTTA GET OUT OF HERE!
WHAT IN THE WORLD DO YOU...
CLICK.
WAIT! THIS'LL DO IT!
EAT FIST, CHUCKIE-BOY!
HOORAY FOR US!

YOU AREN'T CHUCK, OFFICER.
GOOD JOB, BUT WE'RE IN *PERILOUS* DANGER.
WHAT DO YOU MEAN "*WE*", WHITE MAN?
HAVE FUN WITH YOUR NEW FRIEND, BUDDY.
NEW FRIEND? WHAT? HEY!
I BELIEVE HE MEANS ME.
OH, HI... HEH... *NICE* WIENER.
AAAAAAAAAAAGH!!
YOU HEAR A SCREAM?
YEAH, AND A FAMILIAR ONE AT THAT.
WE'VE GOT OTHER THINGS TO WORRY ABOUT.
...IT'S YOUR TURN.
BEM.

...DOUBLE-DOUBLE CHOCOLATE AL-MOND FUDGE-NUT SUPER CRUNCH WITH CHOCOLATE COVERED CHOCO-LATE...
...FUZZY PUPPIES WITH WET NOSES...
...CONSERVATIVE RADIO TALK-SHOW HOST DUNK TANK...
...A COMICS PAGE IN THE WALL STREET JOURNAL...
...GEORGE CLINTON COVERING DUKE ELINGTON...
...AN ALL-EXPENSE-PAID, EIGHT THOUSAND, THREE HUNDRED AND TWENTY-TWO WEEK VACATION...
...NATIONAL FUNK DAY...
...THE POINTLESS EXPLOSIONS NETWORK...
...SATURDAY MORNING CARTOONS IN YOUR P.J.'S AND SLIPPERS...
SUPERGROOVALISTICPROSIFUNKSTICATION
OH, THIS ISN'T WORKING!
EL AANIGOO AHOOT'E.
HE'S *STILL* A BASKET CASE!
YOU SURE YOU CHECKED ALL PSYCHOLOGICAL CURES FOR HIS SPECIES.
JYNNAN TONNYX.
YES AND WE'VE TRIED THEM ALL.
WELL, EXCEPT ONE, BUT I DON'T THINK SMITH WOULD LIKE IT.

IUT 'AY' WA' IUT 'AY' HOM WA'.
LIKE IT?!
IF IT'LL SNAP HIM OUT OF THIS STUPOR, WHAT'S NOT TO LIKE?!
WELL... ALL RIGHT, BUT I KNOW HE'S NOT GOING TO LIKE THIS.
WAIT HERE, I'LL BE RIGHT BACK.
HE'S GONNA KILL ME.
C'MON. UMPH! UMPH, MUMPH!
NA-NU, NA-NU.
GOOD LORD, *CHOKE*!
WHAT IS THAT THING!

YOU 'RE NOT GOING TO USE THAT MONSTROSITY ON HIM?!
YEF, I AM.
ZOOTLEWURDLE
SNORKY!!
HE...HE *LIKES* IT.
OF COURSE HE DOES...
..IT'S HIS SNORKY.
...AND JUST WHAT IS "SNORKY".
IT'S AN EARLY-DEVELOPMENT NEGATIVE-PSYCHOLOGICAL ALLEVIATION ENHANCER.
YOU MEAN, IT'S HIS *SECURITY BLANKET*?!
HA, HA, HA!
MMMMM.

GRUMBLE, GRUMBLE...
LOUSY, STUPID MASTER...
"YOU MUST WAIT FOR THE PROPER TIME, YOUR NON-EARTHLING APPEARANCE WOULD JEOPARDIZE THE WHOLE MISSION."
I'VE GOT YOUR "PROPER TIME" RIGHT HERE!
@#*$!!
BIG, BIG TROUBLE, MR. PHTANG!
GAH!
GOT ME?
MAN, THAT HURTS.
I MEAN... HOW DARE YOU ENTER MY SANCTUM WITHOUT WARNING!
SORRY, BUT A HUB ACCOUNTANT TOOK CHUCK'S HEAD, BOSS.

WHAT?!
EXPLAIN YOURSELF!
WE THOUGHT HE WAS JUST ANOTHER MORONIC FRANCINE SHOW GUEST.
HE GOT THE DROP ON US! WE PUT UP A VALIANT FIGHT BUT HE WAS TOO MUCH! HE WAS UNMERCILESS, MR. PHTANG!
THIS MUST BE DEALT WITH AT ONCE, PERSONALLY, BY ME!
BUT SHOULDN'T WE CALL HEADQUARTERS AND GET INSTRUCTIONS, SIR?
LEAVE THE MASTER OUT OF THIS! I GET TO DO IT! ME, ME, ME!
HEE-HEE.
BESIDES...
...THERE'S NOTHING ON TODAY BUT RE-RUNS.

COO, COO. WHO'S A *GOOD* SNORKY? IT'S *YOU!* YES IT'S...
...YOU?
HEH, HEH.
DON'T WORRY I WON'T TELL ANYONE.
A-*HEM*. MAY I REMIND EVERYONE: EXPRESS TRAIN TO IMPENDING DOOM, NOW BOARDING!
STEALTH-BOTS...
...ON *MY* PLANET!

NEXT: MORE RUNNING AROUND AND SCREAMING AND YELLING AND STUFF.

Chapter Four

showdown!

> Excerpt from the Galactic Central Hub's
> *Accountant Handbook*,
> Published by Grogil and Son.
> Reprinted by permission

Chapter 695- Imposed Limitations on Galactic Central Hub Accountants.

WARNING! READ *VERY* CAREFULLY!

The Interplanetary Accountancy Program is one of the most elite and expensive undertakings developed by the Galactic Central Hub. As such, and because of the now infamous "Fangbort's Fatal Folly" disaster, the Hub sincerely wishes to see that its time and monetary expenditures are used to maximum potential for the benefit of all concerned.

To this end, a microscopic, yet definitely lethal, explosive is attached to every Accountant's surgically implanted translation device. The explosive will be triggered if any of the following three terms of the Accountant's contract are broken:

First, if any attempt to remove the device is made it will detonate, unless you are already dead.

Second, although the mandatory use of the Memwipe-4000 has made it impossible to disclose or use off-world advanced knowledge, Accountants are allowed to retain an advantageous level of information to expedite their studies. However, if this limited information is in any way used to subjugate the inhabitants of your planet, an inboard ethics circuit attached to your translator will trigger the explosive.

Third, if an Accountant tries, for any unauthorized reason, to depart from his assigned planet before his/her/its tour of duty is complete the explosive will be triggered upon leaving the atmosphere of the planet.

If these measures seem harsh and extreme, just remember who's writing the paychecks.

"FINALLY SOMETHING TO DO!"

WE HAVE MET THE ENEMY AND HE IS YOU!

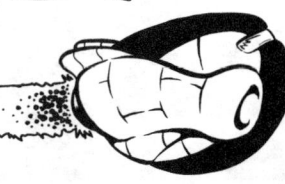

"HEE HEE HEE!"

The Ross Ice Shelf, Antarctica.

PHTANG DID *WHAT?!!*

HE WENT TO "TAKE CARE" OF THE HUB ACCOUNTANT, MR. DABOZ, SIR.
THE INVESTOR S WILL HAVE MY VERY LARGE HEAD OVER THIS!
WHEN DID THE LITTLE TEAL PSYCHOPATH LEAVE?
JUST BEFORE I CONTACTED YOU, SIR.
THEN WE STILL MAY HAVE TIME TO REMEDY THIS.
STAY PUT AND DON'T GO ANY-WHERE!
YES, SIRRRR...ZZZ7
ATTENTION! THIS IS DABOZ. ALL, REPEAT ALL, PERSONNEL TO THE LAUNCH BAY...
...AND BRING THE BIG GUNS.
EVERYONE? BUT, SIR! WHO'S GOING TO MANAGE OPERATIONS?!
THERE WON'T BE ANY OPERATIONS TO MANAGE IF WE DON'T TAKE CARE OF THIS RIGHT NOW, WITH EVERYTHING WE'VE GOT.
I DIDN'T GET THIS LARGE TAKING CHANCES WITH FOES OF SUCH COLD, CALCULATED CUNNING.

THEY PUT ME ON HOLD!
I NEED HELP, NOT A GREATEST HITS MEDLEY!
HELLOOOO, MASSIVELY THREATEN-ING SITUATION. POSSIBLE VERY STICKY DEATH FOR ALL INVOLVED!
PICK-UP! PICK-UP! PICK-UP! PICK-UP! PICK-UP! PICK-UP! PICK-UP!
SIGH.
TURN OUT THE LIGHTS, THE PARTY'S OVER...

GUYS, COME CHECK THIS OUT! I THINK IT MIGHT HELP.
WHAT?!
HUH?!
THANK YOU, RAZ.
DID YOU FIX THE DISPOSAL?
BETTER THAN THAT.
$#@*%!!
IS THAT TOWEL SWEARING?
YES, BECAUSE...
TA-DA!
I THOUGHT YOU COULD USE SOME ANSWERS FROM SOMEONE IN THE KNOW.
THAT'S GREAT RAZ, NO KITCHEN SHOULD BE WITHOUT ONE. BUT HOW IS THIS GOING TO HELP, HE'LL NEVER TALK.
YOU GOT THAT RIGHT! NOW GIVE ME MY BODY BACK SO I CAN TEAR YOU LIMB FROM LIMB, YOU LOSERS!
NO PROBLEM, JUST WATCH.

MR. ROBOT HEAD, ARE YOU GOING TO TALK?
FAT CHANCE, SWEETCHEEKS.
DEFIANT *AND* SEXIST, THAT'LL GET YOU "WHIP".
DÈJÁ VU VU VU VU VU VU VU!
NOW WILL YOU TALK?
IT'LL TAKE MORE THAN THAT, MY NON-FRIEND!
OH GOODY, MY TURN!
LET'S SEE "CHOP", "MIX", "GRATE", OH, LET'S GO STRAIGHT TO "PURÉE".
...ALLRIGHT, ALLRIGHT, ALLRIGHT, ALLRIGHT...
NOW WILL YOU TALK?
YES ALREADY, YOU SADISTIC, SPINNING *MEANY*!
DANG, I DIDN'T GET A TURN.

BUT IT WON'T MATTER *WHAT* I SAY BECAUSE EVERYONE HERE IS A GONER, KA-PUT, KIBOSHED, 86ED, DEAD, *DEAD, DEAD!*
BECAUSE MY *BOSS* WILL BE HERE *ANY MINUTE NOW,* READY TO *KICK* YOUR SORRY *BUTTS* AROUND THE BLOCK! *TWICE! BACKWARDS!*
SO, YOU MIGHT AS WELL JUST DRAW THE CHALK OUT-LINES AND HAVE A LIE-DOWN BECAUSE YOU'RE MORGUE BOUND, YA DINKS!
AND YOUR BOSS IS...?
PHTANG, LAUGHING BOY!
UH-OH.
PHTANG? IS THAT A *NAME?* SOUNDS LIKE A .22 BULLET CAREENING OFF A SKULL PLATE ON A WET AFTERNOON.
HE'S *THE* NUMBER ONE ASSASSIN/MERCENARY/ PSYCHO IN THE GALAXY.
POPS, WHERE'D WE PUT THE CHALK?

ONLY THE PANELISTS ARE SUPPOSED TO BEAT ON EACH OTHER, FRANCINE!
THE HOST LOOKS ON DISAPPROVINGLY, SHE DOES NOT WALLOP THE TAR OUT OF HER GUESTS!
WHAT WERE YOU THINKING?!
STAGE
DRESSING ROOMS
SHE TOUCHED ME.
...AND YOUR CRAZY PEOPLE-PHOBIA MAKES IT ALL RIGHT TO HAVE A LAW SUIT THE SIZE OF OHIO SLAPPED ON OUR...
NOT "PEOPLE", TALK-SHOW GUESTS.
THERE'S A HUGE, UNWASHED, NAUSEATING DIFFERENCE.
SO, UNLESS YOU WANT TO GO BACK TO PRODUCING CABLE ACCESS WEED-ABATEMENT INFOMERCIALS...
...YOU'LL BACK OFF AND LEAVE ME ALONE!
PHILISTINE.
ERK!
UH-OH. THINK FAST.
GUEST ROSTER

HI! I'M YOUR BIGGEST F-F-AN! I L-LOVE YOUR SH-SHOW!
LET M-M-ME SH-SHAKE YOUR G-G-GLAND!
HEEELLP MEEEEE!
SLAM!
FRANCINE!
WHAT?! WHAT?!
STOOPID-D-D T-TRANSLATOR!
THERE IS A HUGE, MUTANT LIZARD-THING IN THERE!
OKAY, CALM DOWN. WE'LL SEE WHAT IT IS.
JAKE. THE DOOR.
DON'T TRY ANYTHING SCUMBAG, YOU'RE IN BIG...WHAT THE...?
IT'S EMPTY.
WHAT! THAT'S IMPOSSIBLE, IT WAS JUST THERE!
FRANCINE, YOU'VE HAD A ROUGH...
DON'T TOUCH ME!!

LOOK, YOU KNOW THIS PHTANG GUY IS COMING, YOU'VE GOT THE ADVANTAGE, SMITH!
RAZ, IT DOESN'T MATTER IF HE R.S.V.P.'S AND BRINGS A ZESTY YET IMPETUOUS BOTTLE OF CHARDONNAY.
I DON'T UNDERSTAND, WHAT'S THE BIG DEAL?
PHTANG IS KNOWN AS "THE LIQUIDATOR." YOU CAN BE ARM-GUARDED, FORCE-FIELD ENCASED, THUG-PROTECTED AND HAVE WEAPONS OUT THE WAZOO ONE MINUTE AND THE NEXT THERE'S NOT EVEN A MICROSCOPIC TRACE LEFT OF YOU!
IF HE'S SO GOOD, WHY'D HE SEND LAME-BRAINED ROBOTS AFTER YOU?
WHY HE'D GO AFTER ME IN THE FIRST PLACE IS THE QUESTION.
IF HE KNEW I WAS HERE, IT WOULD BE EASIER TO AVOID ME THAN RISK A HUB INVESTIGATION OF MY DISAPPEARANCE.
WELL, WE DO HAVE "CHUCK THE AMAZING TWIRLING ENCYCLOPEDIA". WHY NOT ASK HIM?
GOOD IDEA.
HEY, CHUCKIE, GOT A QUESTION FOR YOU...

YOU'LL HAVE TO CATCH ME FIRST!
?
SO LONG, SUCKERS!
AH-HA-HA-HA...
...HA-HA-HA-HA...
...HUH?
OOPS...
HEY!
CRUNCH!
WHAT A DORK.
TRIES TO KILL US, THEN BREAKS OUR BLENDER.
NOW WHAT DO WE...
BEEP!
HELLO? HELLO?
WE'RE HERE!
WELL, WHAT'S SO IMPORTANT, ACCOUNTANT... "JONES"?
WELL, YOU SEE, SIR, MY POPS UNIT AND I RAN ACROSS TWO STEALTHBOTS.
...AND?
...AND THEY TRIED TO KILL US.
IT LOOKS TO ME AS IF THEY FAILED, SO IF YOU'LL KINDLY QUIT WASTING MY TIME...
...SIR, THEY'RE WORKING FOR PHTANG.
SIR?

MR. FLUB??
PH-PHTANG IS ON YOUR LITTLE PLANET THEN?
NO NEED TO WORRY WE'LL HAVE THE HUB ELITE SHOCK TROOPS THERE BEFORE YOU CAN SAY "ZOOP FIPOXAN"!
THANK YOU, SIR! THANK YOU!
WE'RE HERE TO HELP, ACCOUNTANT "JONES".
FLUB OUT.
CALL OUT *ALL* OFFENSIVE PERSONNEL IN THAT SECTOR. THE INSTANT THEY HAVE POSITIVE DNA LOCK ON PHTANG, *DESTROY* THAT AREA.
DON'T RISK TRYING TO SAVE JONES, HE'S TWICE AS GOOD AS DEAD ANYWAY.
SIR, YOU PUSHED THE *AIR-FRESHENER* BUTTON! YOU'RE STILL LINKED!
HEH, HEH...
...OY.
UH-OH.

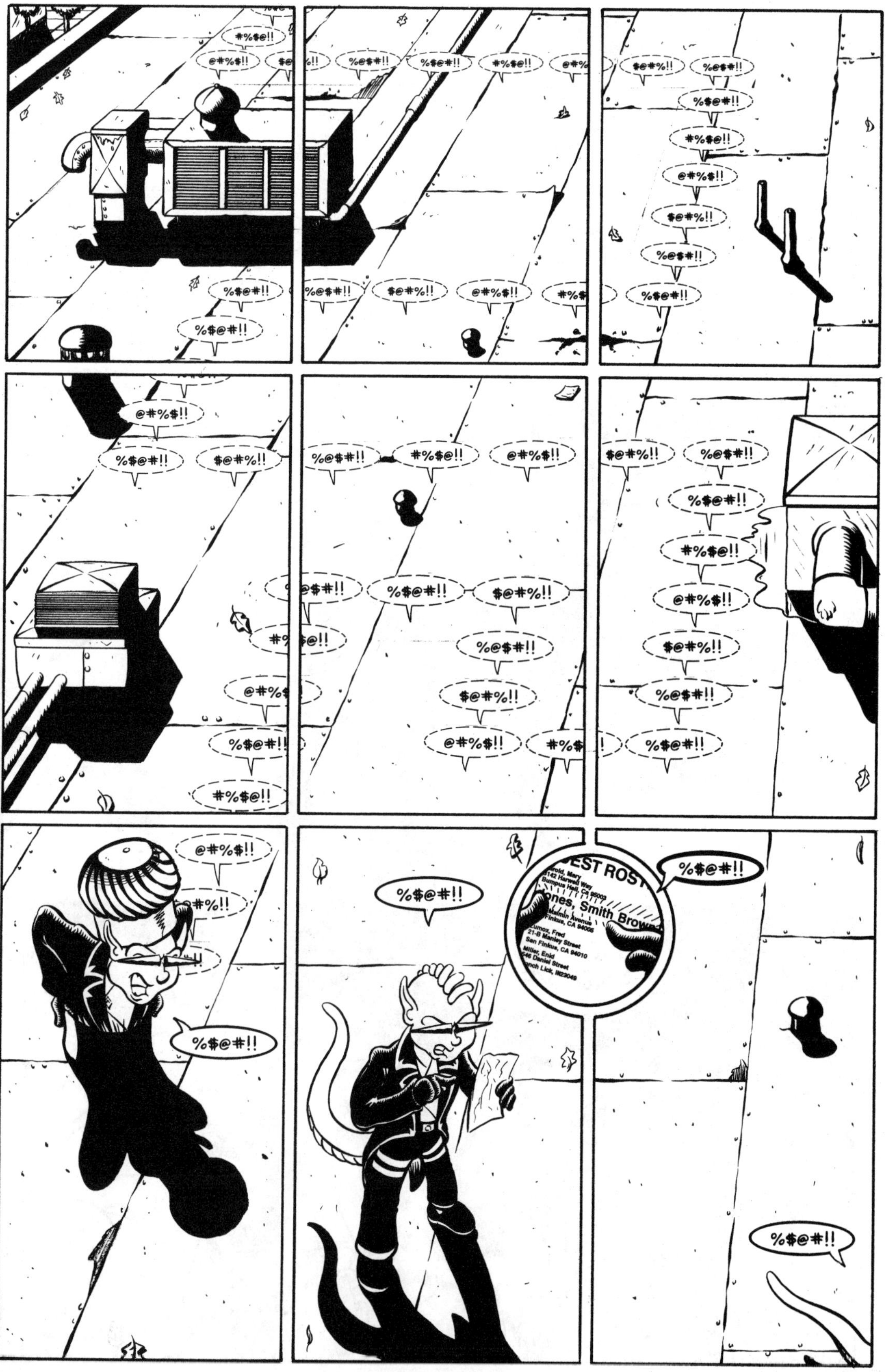

@#%$!!
%$@#!!
%$@#!!
%@$#!!
%$@#!!
#%$@!!
@#%$!!
$@#%!!
@#%$!!
$@#%!!
%@$#!!
%$@#!!
#%$@!!
@#%$!!
$@#%!!
%@$#!!
%$@#!!
@#%$!!
%$@#!!
$@#%!!
%$@#!!
#%$@!!
%@$#!!
#%$@!!
@#%$!!
%$@#!!
%@$#!!
$@#%!!
@#%$!!
$@#%!!
%@$#!!
%$@#!!
#%$@!!
@#%$!!
$@#%!!
%@$#!!
%$@#!!
@#%$!!
%$@#!!
%$@#!!
Jones, Smith Brown
21-B Manley Street
San Finkus, CA 94010
Miller, Enid
%$@#!!
%$@#!!

"...AND EVEN THOUGH HE WAS UNARMED AND CAUGHT BY SURPRISE HE QUICKLY DISPATCHED *BOTH* CHUCK AND MEL."

GASP!

"*GASP!*, MY FRIENDS, IS AN *UNDERSTATEMENT*. THE BOTTOM LINE IS WE HAVE A *MAJOR* THREAT TO OUR BOTTOM LINE! THIS ACCOUNTANT HAS SHOWN ABILITIES BEYOND *ALL* OUR UNDERSTANDING OF WHAT HE *SHOULD* BE ABLE TO DO."

"HOWEVER... WE HAVE THE NUMBERS, WE HAVE THE CUNNING AND, MOST IMPORTANTLY, WE HAVE THE *BIG* GUNS!"

"WILL WE LET HIM STOP US?!"

"WILL OUR HARD WORK BE FOR NOTHING?!"

"WILL WE PREVAIL?!"

"NO! NO! AND YES!"

"NO, NO, AND MAYBE."

C'MON, LET'S GO!
JUST A SECOND, MR. BUTANE'S GIVING US ATTITUDE!
HERE KITTY, KITTY. C'MON YOU FLEA BALL!
DING DONG!
IT'S HIM!
HE DOESN'T MEAN PHTANG, DOES HE?
DIDN'T YOU HEAR THE DARK MENACE IN THE WAY THE DOORBELL RANG?! IT IS HIM!
BUT WHY WOULD HE RING THE DOORBELL? THAT'S STUPID.
THAT'S CONFIDENCE!
OH, COME ON.
SMITH, WHO'S REALLY AT THE...
GOOD LORD, *CHOKE*!
...SMITH?

ALMOST THERE, SIR.
I HAVE A POSITIVE LOCK ON PHTANG'S SHIP.
IT WAS ON A ZIG-ZAG COURSE MOVING NORTHWEST, IT NOW SEEMS TO BE HOLDING A STATIC POSITION.
HE HAD THE SHIP'S COMPUTER FOLLOWING THE STREETS.
SINCE THE SHIP HAS STOPPED WE CAN ASSUME HE'S FOUND THE ACCOUNTANT'S LOCATION.
I SUGGEST WE SPEED UP. OUR CONTINGENCY PLAN DEPENDS ON THE ACCOUNTANT BEING ALIVE...
...AT LEAST FOR A LITTLE WHILE...
...I ALWAYS WANTED TO SAY SOMETHING LIKE THAT.

WHAT DO YOU MEAN HE'S NOT DEAD?!
I DON'T KNOW ABOUT RIGHT THIS *SECOND*, BUT HE *WASN'T* KILLED IN THE APARTMENT.
HOW DO YOU KNOW?!
IF HE WAS DISINTEGRATED, EITHER *ALL* OR *NONE* OF WHAT HE WAS WEARING WOULD BE GONE, DEPENDING ON THE WEAPON.
BUT ONLY WHAT HE HAD ON *TODAY* WAS MISSING. SO HE'S ALIVE...I HOPE.
BUT *WHERE* IS HE?!
I HAVEN'T THE FOGGIE...
TO THE ROOF!

Galactic Central Hub Accountant Handbook, Chapter 1334-B Hostage Crisis Protocol. Step one: Evaluate the captor's mental state.
SO, HOW YA DOIN'?
SHUT UP AND MOVE.
Step two: Make captor see hostages as individuals.
I'M SMITH BROWN JONES. AND YOU MUST BE PHTANG, EH?
SHUT UP AND GET UP THERE.
Step three: Find out the captor's demands.
SAY, HOW 'BOUT A NICE COLD BEER?
SHUT UP AND GET ON THE GRAV-LIFT.
Step four: Comply with demands as reasonably as possible.
I'M ON THAT GRAV-LIFT. BOY HOWDY, JUST CALL ME MR. "DOIN'-WHAT-EVER-YOU-SAY".
SHUT UP AND SHUT UP!

Step five: Having gained trust, use an ongoing dialogue to persuade the captors to release the hostages.
YOU'RE GOING TO KILL ME, AREN'T YOU?!
SHUT UP AND TAKE A RIGHT.
Step six: If release of the hostages is refused, the use of force is cautiously recommended.
IF YOU'LL KINDLY STEP IN HERE.
NO.
Step seven: If situation escalates, see Chapter 2435-D7: First Aid.
OK, HAVE IT YOUR WAY.
KAZAK

AH, GOOD. APOLOGIES FOR THE STUN-RAY, BUT YOU WOULDN'T STOP WITH THE INCESSANT HOSTAGE NEGOTIATION PROCEDURE AND THERE'S NOT MUCH TIME.
IT'S SOUNDPROOF I'M AFRAID. BUILT FOR SPACE FLIGHT, NOT CONVERSATION. ANYWAY, TO ANSWER AN EARLIER QUESTION, I'M *NOT* GOING TO KILL YOU.
I'M MORALLY AGAINST KILLING.
YOU'RE PROBABLY WONDERING *WHY* I FIND KILLING REPUGNANT.
HAVE TO KEEP HIM TALKING.
WELL... IT ALL STARTED WITH MY MOTHER...

IT'S PHTANG'S SHIP ALL RIGHT.
OK, SO... WHAT DO WE DO?
IT'S BUILT TO PROTECT THE GALAXY'S MOST NOTORIOUS *KILLER*.
WITHOUT A BATTALION OF BRAIN-SPLITTER PULPBOTS SET ON "HARANGUE AND DESTROY" IF WE SO MUCH AS SHOUT DEROGATORY REMARKS WE'LL BE REDUCED TO $12.34 OF ORGANIC MATTER.
ALL WE CAN *DO* IS QUIETLY GRIND OUR TEETH AND MUTTER EXPLETIVES WHILE GLARING AT IT INDIRECTLY.
...SO I WAS FORCED TO JOIN THE "ASSASSINS AND PSYCHOS GUILD". *NOT* THE KIND OF BEINGS YOU CAN CASUALLY INFORM THAT YOU'RE A LIFE-LOVING PACIFIST.
NOW, THIS IS WHERE *YOU* COME IN...WITH ALL THE MONEY MOM LEFT ME, I BOUGHT A SMALL, SECLUDED PLANET.
IT'S WHERE I SEND MY "HITS". ON ARRIVAL, THEY'RE PUT IN STASIS UNTIL THE PEOPLE WHO HIRED ME ARE DEAD, THEN THEY'RE FREE TO GO.
...AND THAT'S WHERE *YOU'RE* GOING!
NO, I CAN'T *LEAVE!* MY HEAD'S WIRED TO *BLOW*, YOU DIM LIZARD!
I CAN TELL YOU'RE ECSTATIC, THEY ALWAYS ARE.
WELL... ENJOY THE FLIGHT.

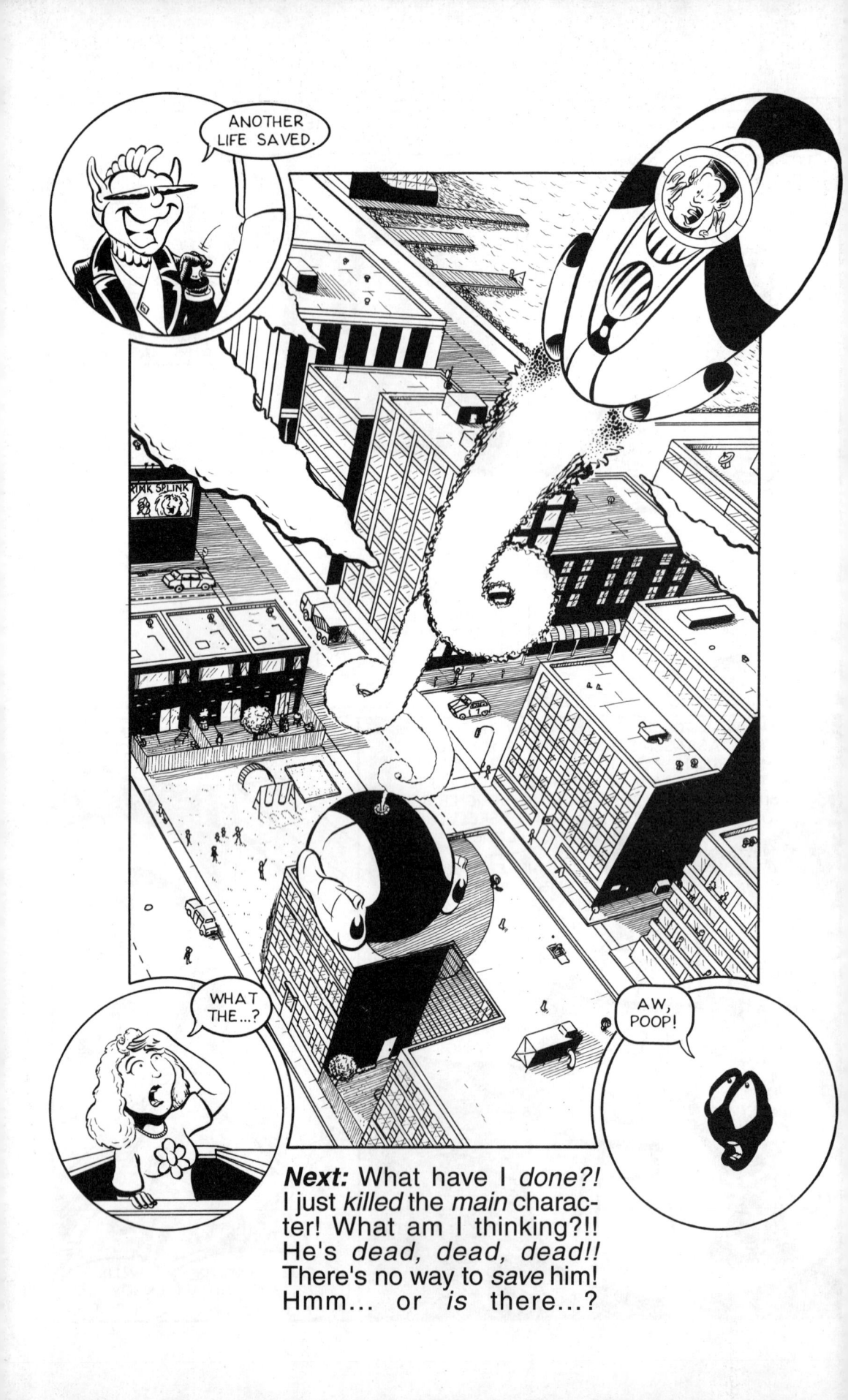

Next: What have I *done?!* I just *killed* the *main* character! What am I thinking?!! He's *dead, dead, dead!!* There's no way to *save* him! Hmm... or *is* there...?

Chapter Five

The SCOURING Eye

Unrepentant Sentient Tuber on Trial for Murder!
"I yam what I yam!" rants Psycho Sweet Potato!

May 17, 1997 $1.05/$1.25 CANADA

REPORTER SAVES EARTH FROM ALIEN FIENDS

OFFICIAL PHOTO!

"Enough with the probing already!" vows *Scouring Eye* Alien Activities Editor!

SO...

...THIS IS DEATH...

...NEVER THOUGHT THE AFTERLIFE WOULD BE AN ALL-ENCOMPASSING BLACK VOID...

...OR THAT IT WOULD TASTE LIKE ASPHALT.

HE'S COMING AROUND, SIR.

AH, GOOD.

HUH?!

UH-OH...

...MAYBE I'M NOT DEAD...

You Got Me Dead to Rites

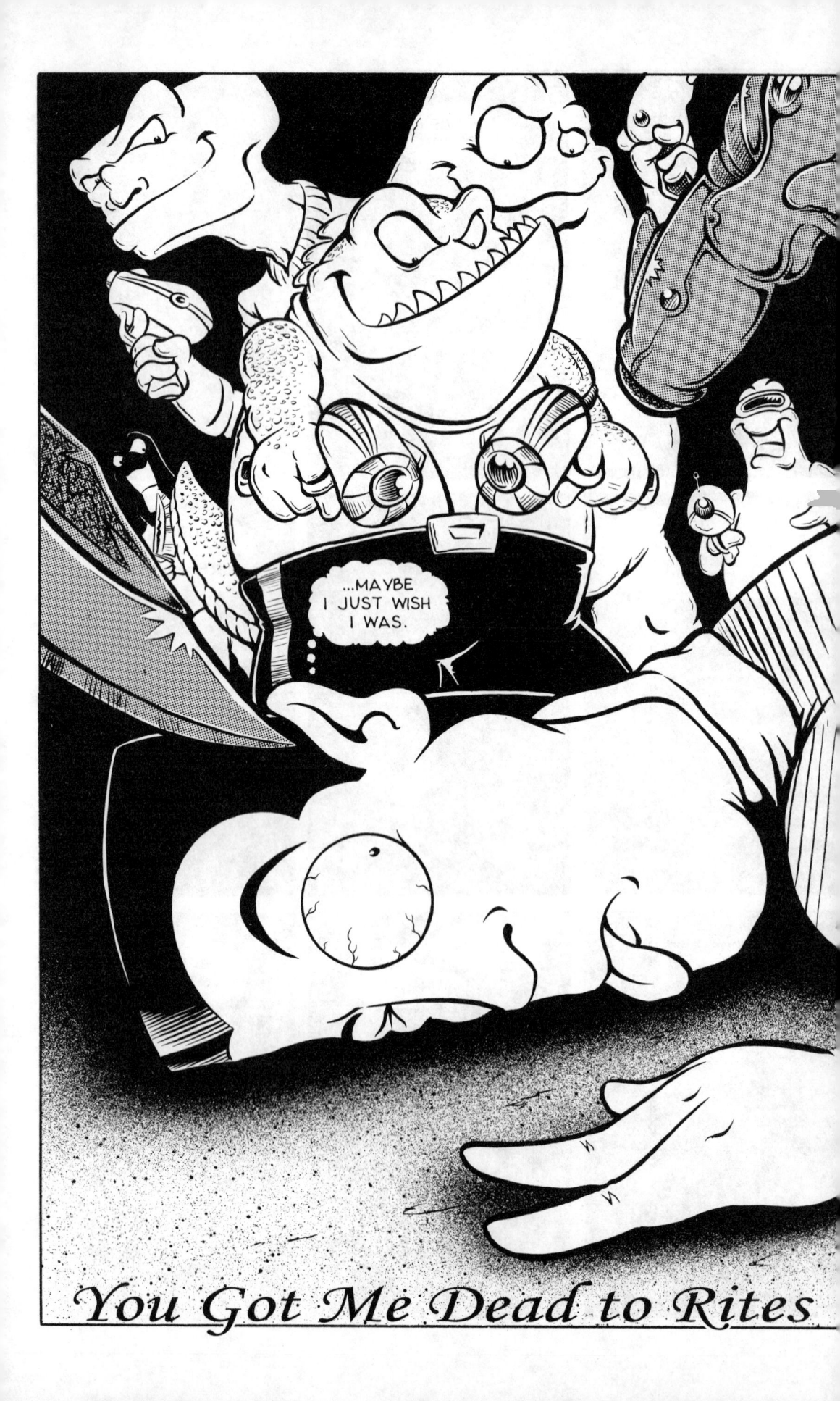

LAD WE INTERCEPTED THE LIFEPOD BEFORE PHTANG COULD DO YOU IN, MR. JONES. HE'S A TAD OVERZEALOUS, BUT HE IS A ARD WORKER. JUST WATCH. PHTANG, PUT HIM WITH HIS FRIENDS!
YES, MASTER.
FRIENDS?! YOU BETTER NOT HAVE HURT THEM OR I'LL... I'LL BE REALLY UNCOOPERATIVE!
MOVE IT SCUM, YOU HEARD MASTER DABOZ.
I AM REALLY SORRY, I DIDN'T KNOW ABOUT THE EXPLODING HEAD THING.
SMITH! YOU ALL RIGHT?
NOT SO TIGHT, YOU GOON.
SAME AS YOU, LOOKS LIKE.
REALLY, REALLY SORRY.
DON'T GET TOO MUCH SLIME ON YOUR HAND HOLDING THIS ONE, RUNGOR.
HEE, HEE.
I'VE ALREADY GOT A RESCUE PLAN IN MOTION, DON'T WORRY.
IS IT AS GOOD AS THE LAST ONE?
STATUS.
ACCOUNTANT... ACCOUNTANT... ACCOUNTANT...
ALMOST READY, SIR.
WHAT ARE YOU GOING TO DO WITH US? IS THAT A HOLOGRAM OF MY HEAD? HEY, YOOHOO, INFO PLEASE!

OH NO. THAT'S *EXACTLY* WHAT SCREWS THESE THINGS UP! I, *SECURE* IN THE KNOWLEDGE THAT I HAVE *DEFEATED* YOU, GLEEFULLY EXPLAIN MY PLOTTINGS *ONLY* TO WATCH YOU BE *MIRACULOUSLY* SAVED AT THE LAST MINUTE AND THEN USE MY ILL-SPOKEN INFORMATION TO *DEFEAT* ME!
AW, C'MON, YOU KNOW YOU WANT TO!
"WANT TO" AND "NEED TO" ARE MUTUALLY EXCLUSIVE IN THIS SITUATION, MY FRIEND.
TELL ME THE PLAN, TELL ME THE PLAN, TELL ME THE PLAN.
I AM NOT TELLING YOU THE PLAN!!
PLEASE, PLEASE, PLEASE!
NO!
PLEASE WITH A CHERRY ON TOP?
NO! NOW BE *QUIET!*
I'LL BE YOUR BEST FRIEND.
I SAID "*NO!*" ARE YOU *TOTALLY* STUPID?
NO, JUST STALLING FOR TIME TO PLAN AN ESCAPE.
GRRRRRRRR!

LISTEN, YOU! *I'M* RUNNING THE SHOW HERE AND *YOU'RE* GOING TO...
HALT, CEASE AND DESIST, *FOUL* ALIENS...
IS *THIS* YOUR PLAN?
HE WAS IN THE PHONEBOOK UNDER HEROIC RESCUE, CAN YOU *BELIEVE* THE LUCK?
HUH? WHAT THE...?!
...OR FACE THE *MYSTERIOUS* WRATH...
...OF *ENIGMAN!!*
I AM ASSUMING, OF COURSE, THAT THE *HIDEOUS* ALIENS ARE THE WRONG-DOERS HERE.
WHAT ARE YOU *TALKING* ABOUT?!!
GOOD, EVIL... THE *ETERNAL* STRUGGLE! SINCE YOU *LOOK* EVIL THEN I ASSUME...
WHAM!

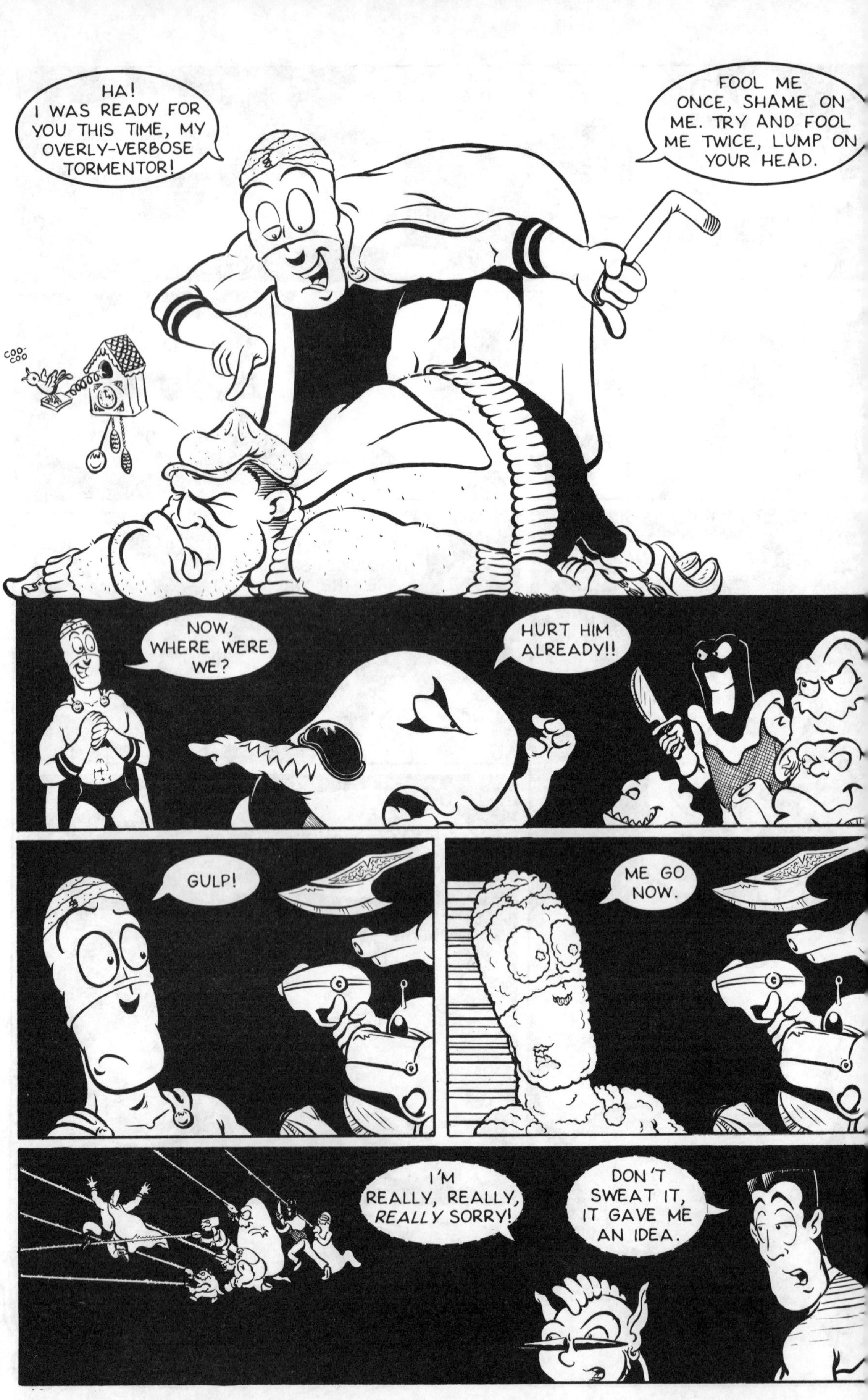
HA! I WAS READY FOR YOU THIS TIME, MY OVERLY-VERBOSE TORMENTOR!
FOOL ME ONCE, SHAME ON ME. TRY AND FOOL ME TWICE, LUMP ON YOUR HEAD.
COO-COO
NOW, WHERE WERE WE?
HURT HIM ALREADY!!
GULP!
ME GO NOW.
I'M REALLY, REALLY, *REALLY* SORRY!
DON'T SWEAT IT, IT GAVE ME AN IDEA.

WOE IS US! IF THAT'S ALL THE HELP MY BRILLIANT STALLING GOT ME, WE'RE DOOMED.
AS IN... "THAT WAS OUR LAST CHANCE FOR AN ESCAPE!"
NICE TRY, BUT WE MONITORED YOUR PA-THETICALLY FRANTIC CALL TO THE HUB, WE KNOW THEY'LL BE ARRIVING SHORTLY, SO WE DON'T HAVE THE TIME TO CHAT.
SEND THE MESSAGE.
YES, SIR.
HUB ATTACK FLEET!
EMERGENCY TRANSMISSION FROM ACCOUNTANT "JONES"...
...I DON'T HAVE MUCH TIME...
...PHTANG HAS FOUND US!
I'M ONLY ALIVE BECAUSE HIS SHIP WAS UNCLOAKED AND APPEARED DAMAGED...
...IT LOOKED LIKE...
LIKE...
GOOD LORD, *CHOKE!*
YEARRGH!!!
IS THAT HOW I SOUND?
I MEAN, THEY'LL NEVER BELIEVE THAT!
THEY WILL WHEN THEY FIND PHTANG'S SHIP, LIMPING ALONG WITHOUT THE USE OF ITS CLOAKING DEVICE.
A RANTING, PLEADING HOLOGRAM OF PHTANG BEGGING FOR MERCY SHOULD FULLY CONVINCE THEM.
LAUNCH THE SHIP.
PROBLEMS SOLVED. WELL, EXCEPT FOR YOURS. YOU'LL BE JOINING US FOR AN EXTENDED VACATION IN THE ANTARCTIC

WAIT! DIDN'T YOU JUST TELL US YOUR PLAN? MEANING WE CAN ESCAPE AND DEFEAT YOU!
NO, MY DEAR, I TOLD YOU *A* PLAN. NOT *THE* PLAN.
OOOO, THE *PLAN*, WHAT'S THAT?
IT'S...
...OH, NO. YOU ALMOST GOT ME THAT TIME. RUNGOR, TAKE THEM...
ALL RIGHT, NOBODY *MOVE!*
NOW WHAT?!!
I'VE GOT ALL OF YOU COVERED!
MAN, THIS IS GREAT!
HEY, IT'S OUR UPTIGHT FRIEND.
HOW'D *HE* GET *HERE?!*

WE'RE ALL GOING TO BE LIKE LITTLE FONZIES...
...AND WHAT'S FONZIE LIKE?
WHAT THE %#*@'S A FONZIE?
NEVER MIND. JUST BUNCH UP. I NEED PICTURES.
WHAT ARE YOU MORONS DOING?!!

POSING.
IS THIS MY GOOD SIDE?
HE'S GOT A GUN.
YOU HAVE GUNS TOO, YOU DIMWITS! *AND*...IF YOU LOOK CLOSELY YOU'LL SEE HE'S GOT *MEL'S* GUN. WHICH IS, IF YOU'LL RECALL, SET ON "*INCREASE INTELLIGENCE*"!
HE COULD FIRE AWAY FOR *HOURS* AND IT WOULD DO *NOTHING* BUT *MAKE SOME FRAZZLE-BLARIN'* IMPROVEMENTS AROUND HERE!
BOMB
NOW GET HIM!!!
NOT AGAIN.
THEY'RE GOING TO *KILL* THAT MAN!
AAAAAAA!!
I THINK I CAN CHANGE THAT.
I HOPE.

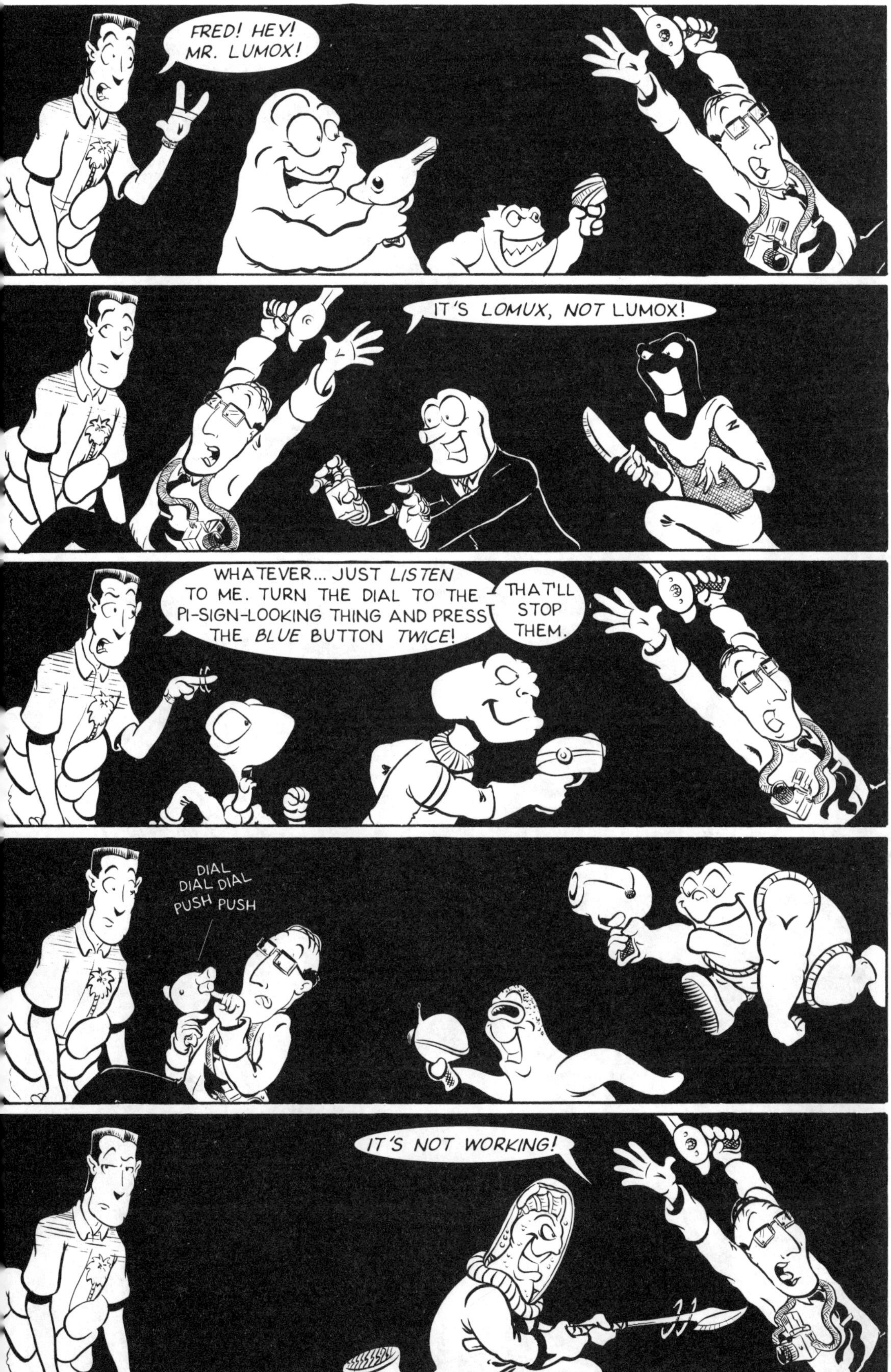
FRED! HEY! MR. LUMOX!
IT'S LOMUX, NOT LUMOX!
WHATEVER... JUST LISTEN TO ME. TURN THE DIAL TO THE PI-SIGN-LOOKING THING AND PRESS THE BLUE BUTTON TWICE!
THAT'LL STOP THEM.
DIAL DIAL DIAL PUSH PUSH
IT'S NOT WORKING!

"TRY POINTING IT AT THEM!!!"

YOU CAN PUT US DOWN NOW...
...WE 'RE WINNING.
IT'S ABOUT TIME.
I'LL TAKE THAT, YOU LOOK A LITTLE SHAKEN.
WH...WHY DID THEY STOP?
BECAUSE THIS IS A GOOZI-2000 CELLULAR DISRUPTOR.
I HAD YOU RESET IT TO "STERILIZE."
...AND WHO'D WANT *THAT*?
BUT...THAT ONE 'S A *ROBOT*...HE DOESN 'T HAVE...
MEL, YOU *MORON*! GET THEM!
HUH... OH, YEAH. OKAY, MR. DABOZ.
POPS, WOULD YOU DO THE HONORS?
MY PLEASURE.

OKAY, THAT ABOUT WRAPS THAT UP.
ANYBODY ELSE WANT TO TRY?
WEEEEEEE-OOOOWEEEEEEE-OOOO
GREAT, THE POLICE.
POPS, HOW LONG UNTIL THEY'RE HERE?
THE DOPPLER EFFECT SAYS... FOUR, FIVE MINUTES
ALL RIGHT EVERYONE!
GRAB YOUR GEAR AND GET ON THE SHIP!

I'M READY TO TELL YOU *THE* PLAN.
NO. THAT'S OK. I LIKE YOUR NON-DISCLOSURE POLICY.
C'MON! LET ME TELL YOU. IT'S REALLY COOL!
LOOK, I'M SETTING THIS THING TO "NO-CHILDREN-THIS-LIFETIME-*OR*-THE-NEXT."
BUT...
ALL RIGHT, ALL RIGHT, *ALL RIGHT!* YOU WIN! *I GIVE UP!*
WHAT'S TO KEEP THEM FROM ESCAPING? WE CAN'T GO WITH THEM. YOUR HEAD WILL EXPLODE AND I CAN'T HOLD THE GUN.
UM... COULD WE HURRY? I'M PROBABLY, SORTA WANTED.

YOU HEARD HIM! THAT'S SPACE-DEPUTY LOMUX TO YOU, NOW GET!
HERE'S THE DEAL, PHTANG. YOU KEEP THESE GUYS ON YOUR PLANET FOR A LONG WHILE AND I'LL FORGET YOU'RE NOT DEAD.
DEAL. DABOZ WILL PROBABLY BE GLAD TO STAY OUT OF THE INVESTOR S HANDS.
EEEEE-OOOOWEEEEE
TO SEAL IT, I'LL JUST TAKE THESE. YOU KNOW, FOR INSURANCE.
YOU SHOULD BE AN EXTORTIONIST.
AND YOU SHOULD BE LEAVING.
SO LONG.
GOOD RIDDANCE.
BYE!
OH... VISIT WAREHOUSE 43B SOMETIME.
ONE PROBLEM DOWN, ONE TO GO.
I'VE GOT THIS ONE. HERE, HOLD HIM FOR ME.
EE-OOOO
I'LL NEED THOSE, THANK YOU. POPS, COME HERE.
EOOOOWEEEEE
EE-OOOOWEEEEEEEE-OOOO
YEAH, RAZ?
YOINK!
EEE-OOOOWEEEEEEEE
KEEP QUIET AND DON'T MOVE.

WHAT'S GOING ON HERE?
IS THERE A PROBLEM, MR. OFFICER, SIR?
WELL UH... MISS, WE GOT A REPORT OF WELL... SPACE ALIENS.
WE'D USUALLY CHALK SOMETHING LIKE THIS UP TO THE MOON OR SWAMP GAS OR SOMETHING...BUT WE'VE BEEN GETTING STRANGE CALLS ALL NIGHT.
ASIDE FROM MY UNCONVINCINGLY DRESSED FRIEND HERE, I DIDN'T SEE ANY AT THE COSTUME PARTY WE WERE JUST AT, BUT WE LEFT EARLY.
SINCE YOU'RE OUT HERE *ANYWAY*, COULD YOU DO ME A TEENSY FAVOR?
OUR PLEASURE, MISS.
OUR FRIEND IS A LITTLE TIPSY AND HE'S KINDA HEAVY, COULD YOU...?
MMPRH... TIPSHY.
YOU SURE YOU AND YOUR FRIEND DON'T NEED A RIDE ALSO?
WE LIVE CLOSE BY.
WELL, OK... BUT BE CAREFUL, THIS IS A ROUGH NEIGHBORHOOD.
DON'T WE KNOW IT.
I'M KEEPING THE GLASSES.
DO I HAVE TO COME OUT NOW?

...and that's pretty much it. Hyperbully sent us a "thank you for not leaving me unconscious in the bowery" card. He even forgave us for sending his roommate, Mr. Lumox (can you believe it!), into outer space and said his *new* roomie was working out even better.
IT'S GOING... IT'S GOING... *IT'S GONE!!!*
D.U.M. EQUIPMENT
OUTS VISITOR
CHIPS
HB

The assassin formerly known as Phtang and our up-tight-until-recently friend are taking a tour of various exotic locales ...the city-state of "Yipyipyipyippee" was their last know destination. They have, with good reason, turned off all communication devices.
THIS IS SO COOL!

Right after leaving Earth, Daboz and company quickly agreed to a long nap, about a millennium or so. Which, although fortunate for them, left us with many questions unanswered.

As for Raz, Pops and myself, we're still confused as all get out, due to said questions...

HOW'D *THAT* VIRUS WORK?

STILL BEING BLOCKED. DABOZ'S SECURITY IS *IMPECCABLE*, WE'LL BE LUCKY TO LEARN ANYTHING.

WELL, WHAT *DO* WE KNOW?

WE KNOW PHTANG HAS PILES OF VIDEOTAPES FILLED WITH INANE TALK SHOWS AND THAT CHUCK AND MEL WERE SENT TO THESE SHOWS WITH GUNS SET TO INCREASE THE INTELLIGENCE OF THE MORONIC GUESTS. BUT, WHY?

HMMMMM...

"THE 'LESS-COUTH' TEND TO CARRY-ON ABOUT INEXPLICABLE PHENOMENA."

OK. SMARTENING UP STUPID HUMANS *WOULD* ALLOW ALIEN SPECIES MORE COMFORT IF THEY WERE TO *VISIT* EARTH. BUT, THAT'S NOT ALLOWED UNTIL EARTH IS PART OF THE GALACTIC CENTRAL HUB CONGRESS.

TWO BIRDS WITH ONE STONE? MORE INTELLIGENCE, LESS CARRYING-ON, THEREFORE, QUICKER ACCEPTANCE.

...BEEP...
...BEEP...
...BEEP...
...BEEP...
...BEEP...
...BEEP...

WE GOT SOMETHING... LOOKS LIKE AN UNPROTECTED GRAPHICS FILE IN A LOWER SYSTEM.

EARTHWORLD
The Largest Resort in the Galaxy!

(Panel 1)
— DOWN LOAD IT TO THE PRINTER. MAYBE IT WILL TELL US *SOMETHING*.
— ...AND TRANSLATE IT INTO ENGLISH FOR THOSE OF US WHO ARE ALIEN LANGUAGE IMPAIRED.

(Panel 2)
— HA, HA, HA, HA!

(Panel 3)
— WHAT? WHAT IS IT?!
— YEAH, DOES IT TELL US ANYTHING?

(Panel 4)
— I THINK IT SAYS IT ALL...

Crazy Uncle Daboz says:
— HEY, EVERYONE! C'MON DOWN, THE ATMOSPHERE IS FINE!

Yes! Now you too can stay at my newest fun-filled paradise! You thought *ContinentCountry* and *HemisphereLand* were big! Well you ain't seen *nothing* yet! My new resort *EarthWorld* is compatible with 8,675,271,477,147,970,006 beings! That's a whopping 93% of all Hub citizens and that probably means *you*! We've got seas, deserts, tundras, jungles, plains... a friendly climate for one and all! So, don't delay... there's a whole *world* waiting!

SUPER DUPER DOUBLE SPECIAL SMITH BROWN JONES EXTRA BONUS PAGES

WARNING!!

The following bonus pages contain pictures of Smith Brown Jones and cohorts having way too much fun on vacation in Las Vegas and their subsequent visit to Area 51.

Kiwi Studios accepts no responsibility for any bodily damage occurring from chuckles, belly laughs, guffaws, titters or giggles suffered during the perusal of these pages.

Our cat, Fluffy-Muffin Cocoa-Butter, (model for Smith's cat, Mr. Butane) looking fat and sad because we're leaving for our fabulous week long vacation in Las Vegas! Seconds after the picture was taken, she hacked up a doozy of a hairball in protest.

"The Strip" as seen from the Stratosphere. Some of the casinos pictured include the Excalibur, the Mirage, Circus Circus, the Luxor, Treasure Island, New York New York, the MGM Grand and a couple dozen more. Seconds after the picture was taken, I sneezed, almost falling to my death.

Smith in the middle of the desert, Las Vegas shining greedily in the far distance. Seconds after the picture was taken, he panicked, thought he would die of thirst and tried to drink the wiper fluid out of the rent-a-car. He calmed when we handed him a Snapple.

Doin' a little celebrity stalking. Smith lurks in the yuccas outside of magician Penn Gillette's house. (His parents live in the normal ranch house on the left, while he lives in the "post-modern penitentiary" side grafted, Frankenstein-like, onto it.) Seconds after the picture was taken, Penn's partner, Teller, peered over the wall and shouted some rather rude obscenities at us.

EXTRATERRESTRIAL HIGHWAY
357

Astrophotographer and flying object (unidentified or otherwise) expert Chuck Clark being interviewed by a film crew from the Discovery channel. Seconds after the picture was taken, Chuck identified a bird flying overhead (which we all thought was an F-16) as a B1RD-RAVEN.

Activity at the gate to Area 51! A well-armed guard checks security passes before letting an official vehicle into "Dreamland". Seconds after this picture was taken, a cigar-shaped craft also had its pass checked. Then the alien occupants mooned us and flew off at over 900 miles per hour.

To the left, hidden by the mountain range, is Groom Lake and Area 51. The signs that Smith is standing by read: "WARNING. Restricted Area. It is unlawful to enter this area without permission of the Installation Commander. While on this installation all personnel and the property under their control are subject to search. Use of deadly force authorized," and "Photography of this area is prohibited." Seconds after this picture was taken, we had to dodge a hail of gunfire. Smith screamed like a little girl.

Located in Rachel (the closest town to Area 51), the Little A'Le'Inn is a motel, bar and restaurant that plays host to both neighborly locals and U.F.O. buffs from around the world. The owners, Pat and Joe Travis (really friendly folks), host a biannual "U.F.O. Friendship Camp-out" and have entertained celebrities such as Montel Williams, Larry King and the makers of Independence Day, who left the time capsule/monument pictured in upper left corner of this postcard. You can contact the Little A'Le'Inn at (702)729-2515.

Smith bellies up to the bar at the Little A'Le'Inn and orders seventeen "bahama mamas". Seconds after the picture was taken, owner Joe Travis (the blurry gentleman to Smith's right) smartly says he has to go feed the pigs.

Three cartoonists and two (one alien, one not) accountants. From left to right: Andy Hartzell (creator of *Bread and Circuses*), myself, Smith, my lovely fiancée Terry and F. Andrew Taylor (creator of *Beer and Roaming in Las Vegas*.) Seconds after the picture was taken we were signed by a modeling agency.

Smith starts his shopping spree at the Little A'Le'Inn's souvenir stand. Seconds after the picture was taken, a large chunk of cash was abducted from my wallet.

Although we saw nothing resembling a U.F.O. on our trip, upon returning home F.M.C.B. assumed this rather alien position (yes, those are her back legs up by her ears). Seconds after the picture was taken, we laughed our travel-weary heads off.

Smith Brown Jones and Pops   by Scott Adams

Chuck and Mel by Linda Medley

Razals Salazar by Molly Kiely

Phtang

by F. Andrew Taylor

Daboz by Greg Espinoza

What if Smith Brown Jones comics were forbidden?

utrageous? Sure it is, but the works of many comic book professionals have been seized and sometimes
nned by the real life thought police.

e Comic Book Legal Defense Fund was founded to fight these threats. In the last five years, the CBLDF
s spent over $200,000 defending First Amendment rights in the comic book industry. We have successfully
ended or deterred over a dozen threats to comic book artists, publishers, and retailers from over-zealous
ice departments, prosecutors, and would-be censors.

ase help us continue our mission to fight censorship by making a donation. With your support, the
LDF can continue to champion comic book professionals' freedom of speech. After all, it's the thought
ice that should be banned!

---

and mail)

_____ Yes! I want to help fight censorship in the
mic book industry. Enclosed is my tax-
ductible contribution of:

_____ $15   _____ $50
_____ $25   _____ other

ease add my name to your mailing list and
nd me more information:

me: _____
ldress: _____
ty/State: _____ Zip: _____

THE COMIC BOOK LEGAL DEFENSE FUND

Mail donations and inquiries to:
CBLDF • P.O. Box 693
Northampton, MA 01061
1-800-992-2533
e-mail: 102437.1430@compuserve.com